Three Cheers for Lucia!

A Mapp and Lucia Novel

and sequel to *Au Reservoir*

Ian Shepherd

Published in 2015 by Kingswood Publishing, Norwich

A CIP catalogue record for this title is available from the British Library.

ISBN: 978–1514721148

Introduction

In a seemingly unshockable world, shocks of a literary nature are few and far between. However, just last year, loyal fans of E. F. Benson's inspired and enduring comic creation – Lucia Pillson – were left reeling over Guy Fraser-Sampson's decision to 'kill her off' in his final Mapp and Lucia novel *Au Reservoir*.

First introduced to the public in 1920, Emmeline Lucas, later Pillson and known to all her friends as Lucia, captured the imagination of readers both young and old. Her adversary, Elizabeth Mapp appeared shortly afterwards in 1922. However, it was not until 1931 that they joined forces in Benson's fourth novel of the series – a comic partnership that is, arguably, one of the greatest in twentieth century English literature. 'We will pay anything for Lucia books' was the famous *Times* advertisement placed collectively by a notable quartet of desperate fans: Nancy Mitford, W. H. Auden, Gertrude Lawrence and Noël Coward in the 1940s.

Benson's final book *Trouble for Lucia* was published shortly before his death in 1940 and one would assume that, had he lived, he would have continued the narrative, such was its popularity. There is no indication in the text that this was to be the final book of the series.

Over forty years later, the fledgling Channel 4 commissioned London Weekend Television to make *Mapp and Lucia*, brilliantly adapted from Benson's final three books by Gerald Savory and featuring sparkling on-screen performances by Geraldine McEwan as Lucia and Prunella Scales as Mapp. Such was the success of the first series (a second series followed a year later in 1986) Black Swan republished the original books. Also worthy of note are Aubrey Woods adaptations of several of the books which were broadcast on BBC Radio 4 in the 1980s.

In this wake of resurgent interest in Benson's characters, Tom Holt wrote two subsequent novels, again published by Black Swan in 1985 and 1986, which perfectly captured the spirit of the originals, moving the narrative to the 1939-45 War and afterwards. Guy Fraser Sampson began his trilogy of novels in 2008 with *Major Benjy*. Six years later in *Au Reservoir*, the residents of Tilling are facing post-war rationing.

In this final book, Sampson introduces some 'real life' characters and introduces the delicious prospect of Lucia becoming Lady Pillson. We also learn that she is far more wealthy than we had previously assumed. Such a shame then to cut her down!

In wishing to continue the story, I have taken the liberty of altering Sampson's final chapter. Thus, rather than dying (and it must be conceded that Sampson's narrative is both heartfelt and moving), Lucia clings on to life – awaiting a stronger dose of pencillin.

Whilst writing this novel, three significant events occurred. Firstly, the BBC aired a new version of *Mapp and Lucia*, adapted by Steve Pemberton and starring

Miranda Richardson as Mapp and Anna Chancellor as Lucia. Universally praised by the critics, the series introduced Benson's Tilling to a whole new generation. Secondly, to coincide with this, the BBC also released its 1985 Radio 4 dramatisation of *Queen Lucia* starring Barbara Jefford on CD and thirdly, the sad news that Geraldine McEwan – the definitive Lucia – had died in January 2015 was announced.

I do hope that you enjoy reading the further adventures of Lucia and Georgie, Mapp and the Major and their wonderful circle of friends. If I have captured just a tiny fragment of E. F. Benson's spirit, then I shall be happy!

Ian Shepherd

Acle, Norfolk.

Chapter 29

… Doctor Kendrick was a young man, and clearly nervous. He opened his desk drawer and took out a rather crumpled bag of Imperial mints. He offered Georgie one with a slightly trembling hand.

'Not at the moment, thank you,' said Georgie as the doctor took one of the said mints and popped it into his mouth.

'How is she?' asked Georgie, nervously.

'The penicillin does not appear to be having a great effect, Mr. Pillson. It's really quite serious.'

There was an audible 'crack' as Doctor Kendrick bit his mint into two.

'If she had just seen the doctor a few days earlier then the septicaemia would have been less invasive.'

There was a long pause. Georgie's mind was racing but he could think of nothing to say.

'I have been in touch with Great Ormond Street again,' continued the doctor, 'and they have agreed to send down a stronger batch of penicillin. It should arrive this afternoon.'

'Will it do any good?' asked Georgie.

'We can only hope, Mr. Pillson. And pray.'

Chapter 1

'Wake up Lucia,' whispered Georgie gently into his wife's ear, as he had done religiously every morning, afternoon and evening for the last fortnight. Lucia lay there, in the hospital bed, frail yet serene in her own enclosed world, surrounded by flowers, cards and uneaten baskets of fruit – gifts sent by dear friends from Tilling, Riseholme and beyond. Even Noël Coward, on hearing her plight, had sent a signed photograph with a sympathetic message on the back. It had been given pride of place amongst the cards, the beaming smile slightly obscured by a drooping tulip.

'Wake up Lucia,' Georgie whispered once more. However, as always, she never stirred. In fact, one had to study her whole being extremely closely in order to see even the faintest signs of life. A periodic slight rise and fall of the bedcovers was the only visible indication that Lucia was still breathing. This had been the position ever since she had been given the stronger dose of penicillin by Doctor Kendrick. He had told Georgie that the treatment was not proven in very serious cases and to prepare himself for a long period of uncertainty. Indeed, the doctor warned, Lucia might never wake up.

Although Georgie was not an overly religious man, he felt some comfort in the fact that the Padre had said prayers for Lucia during services at Church for the last two weeks. Amongst the residents of Tilling there was a great sense of agitation and worry as the perennial question 'Any news?' was answered, usually by Grosvenor or Foljambe, with the solemn reply 'Sorry, no news to report today.' The Mapp-Flints, Wyses, Bartletts, Diva and Quaint Irene carried on their daily marketing, knowing full well that Lucia's condition was extremely serious.

As he was now prone to do, Georgie took hold of Lucia's delicate hand and immediately noticed a slight warmth that had been absent since she had slipped into a coma. Then, to his astonishment, there was the tiniest movement – not quite a squeeze – but something tangible all the same. With a forced sense of calm, he signalled for the nurse to fetch the doctor.

After what seemed like an age (though it had been less than five minutes), Doctor Kendrick arrived. He felt for Lucia's pulse, declaring that it did indeed appear stronger than before.

'Mr. Pillson, we're certainly not out of the woods yet but I think we are making progress. Nurse, take a pulse every half hour and increase fluids.'

The doctor turned to Georgie.

'There is a chance that Mrs. Pillson might possibly wake up in the next few days. If this happens she will be very weak and disorientated. And as to her state of mind?' The doctor paused. 'She will need plenty of time to recover and there must be absolutely no distractions whatsoever.'

Georgie gratefully shook the doctor's hand.

'I'll stay here as long as I can until she wakes!' he replied.

For three days, anticipation that Lucia might wake up was misplaced and a feeling of dread began to overtake Georgie's emotions as he pondered the nature of her recovery. Would she return as the Lucia he knew so well and loved, or might she be just a shadow of her former self? Would she still be able to play Beethoven? Would she even remember her own name and that she had a husband called Georgie? The thought of spending the rest of his days nursing an invalid filled him with horror.

The next day Georgie arrived at the hospital rather later than usual. Cadman, the chauffeur, had discovered a puncture earlier that morning and the Rolls could not be used until he had changed the wheel. Being a meticulous worker, Georgie knew that he would have to wait until Cadman had fully completed the procedure and tested the traction before embarking on the journey.

Once at the hospital, he said his customary 'Hello' to the nurse and sat down in the high-back chair which he had had delivered to the hospital from Mallards. If he was to sit at Lucia's bedside all day, every day, then he might as well do so in some comfort. The nurse reported that Mrs. Pillson had enjoyed a peaceful night and that her pulse remained strong.

'I'm sure that it won't be long now, sir. Now and again she moves her head from side to side and that's always a good sign,' and she smiled reassuringly.

Later on, Georgie must have drifted off to sleep as it was now past four in the afternoon and he was awoken by the sound of the tea trolley clattering in the nearby corridor. Although the lady who dispensed the tea had boasted to Georgie that it was her brew that cured most of the patients, Georgie, having tasted it just once, was unable to agree – a foul, dark liquid that had had ruinous effects upon his digestion. Knowing that he would be spending a considerable time at the hospital, he had instructed Foljambe to make up a small box of refreshments which could be stored in the rather distressed cabinet next to Lucia's bed. Foljambe had included a small box of tea bags which Twistevant's, Tilling's general store, had just started to sell. They were pronounced 'A miracle!' by the tea lady.

He looked at Lucia. She seemed to be making blinking movements, though her eyes remained closed. Georgie wondered for how long this had been happening and felt a sudden sense of guilt that he had been asleep and had perhaps missed other vital signs of recovery. This blinking lasted for about half an hour and then suddenly, almost comically, Lucia slowly opened one eye. She turned her head slightly, gradually focussed on her husband and began to smile.

'Oh Lucia! You're back!' Georgie exclaimed. 'We all thought you were going ...'
Georgie's voice trailed off as he frantically searched for his silk handkerchief in a failed attempt to stop the tears from rolling down his cheeks. Slightly flustered by this outward sign of emotion, Georgie made for the door.
'I must fetch the doctor,' he called back to his wife.

Doctor Kendrick returned enthusiastically to Lucia's bedside to administer a series of tests, most of which, from the nodding of the doctor's head, she seemed to be passing with flying colours. Georgie winced as she was prodded and poked but Lucia herself remained impassive.

'Is everything in order?' asked Georgie.

'It appears so, Mr. Pillson. Obviously, Mrs. Pillson is weak but she appears to have suffered no lasting physical consequences. I suggest we keep her in hospital for the next week in order to build up her strength and keep an eye on her.'

'Keep an eye on me Doctor?' croaked Lucia.

'She can speak!' exclaimed Georgie, with genuine excitement.

'You've had a very nasty illness, Mrs. Pillson,' replied the doctor, speaking very slowly and carefully, as if addressing a small child. 'You have been unconscious for over two weeks.'

'Yes, Lucia,' confirmed Georgie, 'That wretched insect bite!'

'Fetch some more pillows for Mrs. Pillson, Nurse. She should be able to sit up now.'

The nurse brought Lucia an additional two pillows and carefully made Lucia more comfortable. Lucia was in her own room, giving her a modicum of privacy befitting an ex-Mayor of Tilling and past benefactress of the hospital before it became part of the National Health Service.

'I'll go to the kitchens and see if I can find you something to eat, Mrs. Pillson. I'm sure you must be hungry,' and she moved off in the direction of the hospital kitchen, returning a couple of minutes later with a streaming bowl of soup. Georgie looked at the thin, insipid liquid as the nurse placed the tray on Lucia's lap. Watery green in colour, it could have been pea, perhaps celery or even cabbage soup. To Georgie it looked particularly unappetising.

'That looks delicious, Lucia,' said Georgie, unconvincingly. After a short pause, and much to Georgie's surprise, Lucia picked up the spoon and slowly but surely emptied the contents of the bowl.

Georgie was beaming and felt like applauding the empty vessel.

'Oh Lucia! I must tell all our friends that you are on the road to recovery.'

Lucia gave Georgie a firm stare and grabbed his hand.

'Not yet, Georgie. When I am ready,' and she squeezed his hand, as if sealing the deal.

The following day, Georgie went to the hospital in the early afternoon. Before luncheon he had visited the High Street – the first time for several days, and had successfully avoided meeting anyone and thus did not have to answer the question 'Any news?' He so wanted to tell everyone that Lucia was on the mend but had made a promise to Lucia that he would say nothing – for the moment, at least.

On entering Lucia's room, he was surprised to see her sat up, nose firmly in a copy of *Harper's Bazaar*, a cup of tea obscuring the wistful smile of Noël Coward. As soon as she heard him come in, she put down the magazine and beckoned for him to sit down on the chair beside her bed.

'Feeling so much better today, Georgie,' she said, her voice stronger and firmer than before. 'I've just had some soup.'

'Soup? What kind?' he enquired.

'Green soup, Georgie! Could be anything! Any news, Georgie?'

Georgie began to tell Lucia all the Tilling news and gossip. Not that there had been much of the latter given the recent circumstances and subdued atmosphere. Lucia was gratified to hear that the Padre had said regular prayers for her and was especially moved to hear that Quaint Irene had posted several illustrated poems through Mallards' letterbox, with titles such as *Heaven Can't Have My Angel Yet* and *Desolation in Tilling.* It was Georgie's opinion that Irene, now a feted artist, was no poetess. Diva had postponed the introduction of coconut macaroons to the menu of the tea-shop as a rather bewildering mark of respect and the Wyses had taken to walking to the High Street so that Susan could 'share the pain' that Lucia was undoubtedly suffering.

'Nodoubt a temporary measure, Georgie!' quipped Lucia. 'And the Mapp-Flints?' she enquired. 'Has Elizabeth been taking advantage of my absence?'

'Quite the opposite, in fact, Lucia. She has been very quiet. Withers told Grosvenor last week that Mapp has hardly ventured out of Grebe since you were admitted to hospital.'

'Perhaps I judge her too harshly, Georgie?'

As Lucia lay in bed, thoughts of her own mortality and near-death experience were never far from her mind. She remembered her spiritual connection with Blue Birdie, the beloved budgerigar of Susan Wyse, which had sadly passed away but whose body Susan had desperately clung on to. With Lucia's assistance it had dematerialised and was, even now, still flying on the astral plane. The fact that Lucia had, in fact, secreted it away in a black japanned box marked 'Museum', on the insistence of Mr. Wyse who feared his wife was starting to go 'dotty', was not of any consequence.

Lucia had read about near-death experiences in several journals and the Guru at Riseholme had talked in depth about them, much to Lucia's facination. He had actually claimed to have suffered four of them. 'You must be more careful!' was Lucia's response. The fact that the Guru was discovered to be a light-fingered curry chef rather than a true follower of 'the way' seemed immaterial in present cicumstances. Lucia so wanted to tell Georgie that she had seen a great white light at the end of a long tunnel, where she had seen Pepino, in his prime, calling for her. She had wanted to join him but something intangible had held her back – perhaps that was Georgie?. But, in truth, there had been nothing. A void. Emptiness. On entering hospital, she recalled being put into bed, being given a pill to swallow and then nothing. The next thing she remembered was seeing Georgie, blurred yet instantly recognisable at her bedside, tears streaming down his face.

With no visitors, apart from Georgie, of course, Lucia spent much time engaged in conversation with the hospital workers. Her day nurse, who Lucia quickly found out was called Eliza, had three grown-up children and held the common belief that even complete strangers would find the exploits of her offspring as engaging and entertaining as she did herself. Cyril, the hospital handyman, had repaired a stiff door handle one day and changed a tap washer the next. Spending just a few minutes on the prescribed jobs, he had extended his visits by sitting down in Georgie's chair and bemoaning the fact that Winston Churchill was no longer in charge of the country.

Milly, the ancillary, lived on the municipal estate and had recently married. She was still living, along with her husband, in her parents' house, due to a shortage of housing in Tilling and a meagre combined income. Unfortunately, her husband, who had been a bus driver before the War, had lost the lower half of his left leg just a month before the ceasing of hostilities.
'I says he was just unlucky, Mrs. Pillson and he turns to me and says the opposite – that he is very lucky to have just lost a bit of his leg!'
Despite the fitting of a prosthetic limb, he had been unable to get his old job back and had several casual jobs

since. Lucia made a mental note to contact Milly once she had left hospital.

Milly, it turned out, was a bit of a bookworm. A regular visitor to the library, she was also happy to accept hand-me-down books from fellow hospital workers, peruse the stalls at local jumble sales and very occasionally visited the large bookshop in Hastings to buy one of the latest novels.

'Not that I've got a lot to spare at the end of the week, Mrs. Pillson, but reading is my escape,' she told Lucia. 'I've just finished a new book by Nancy Mitford – I'll bring it in for you.'

Lucia was not sure whether the kind of books Milly liked would be exactly to her own taste. However, she responded to the offer enthusiastically and for the rest of the week, Lucia read *Love in a Cold Climate* voraciously. Surprisingly aligning herself with the young heroine, Polly, rather than her mother, Lady Montdore, it was a thrilling read and brightened up each day for several hours, though the book was firmly hidden under the pillow when Georgie visited.

Doctor Kendrick took Lucia's pulse for a final time.
'Very strong, Mr. Pillson.'
He still had that annoying habit of addressing Georgie rather than the patient. Lucia might have said something to him on that matter in different circumstances but she was extremely grateful for his care.
'She's certainly strong enough to go home now though another week of rest would be beneficial.'

At that, he signed a form, handed in to the nurse, shook Georgie's hand and smiled at Lucia.

'Thank you, Doctor,' said Lucia as he made his way to the next patient.

'Well, Georgie, back to dearest Mallards.'

'Oh I can't wait to let everyone know that you are back home, Lucia,' replied Georgie.

Lucia looked alarmed.

'No visitors yet, Georgie. I need to feel fully restored.'

'But what shall I say, Lucia? You know how desperate they all are to hear that you are better. Only yesterday I had to jump into an alley just to avoid Diva Plaistow on the High Street. Algernon Wyse has started to telephone Mallards every evening at six o' clock sharp to check your progress.'

'Just one more week, Georgie. Tell them that I am still at the hospital,' and she gave a wistful smile. 'You'll do that for *ickle* Lucia?

Georgie dearly wanted to protest, but, as ever, succumbed to his wife's wishes.

Chapter 2

Elizabeth Mapp-Flint was in the kitchen at Grebe, peeling crab apples, ready for an afternoon of jam-making. Normally an enjoyable activity, she was feeling rather downcast. Withers had been given most of the day off as Mapp preferred to have the entire kitchen to herself when preserving and pickling – a necessary task which supplemented her modest income.

This year her crab apple tree had been unusually generous and she estimated that she would be able to make at least three dozen jars of crab apple jelly – two dozen of which she would sell to Twistevant's, Tilling's general store, reserve six for Christmas gifts and use the rest for domestic consumption. She already had a cupboard full of strawberry, raspberry and gooseberry jam. Unfortunately, the batch of blackberry preserve had been completely ruined as she had, perhaps unwisely, left the Major in charge of the simmering pot as she walked into Tilling. He had dozed off, newspaper and empty glass in hand, leaving the blackberry mixture on the boil until Mapp returned, two hours later. Her best copper pan, bequeathed by her Aunt Caroline, had been ruined in addition to its contents.

Mapp was just adding sugar to the crab apples when the telephone rang. She shouted for Benjy to answer it. Shortly, the Major entered the kitchen.
'That was Georgie. He would like to see us for an important announcement at two o' clock sharp… looks

18

like it's all over, Elizabeth.'

Ever since Lucia's admission into hospital, Mapp had considered the possibility that Lucia might not recover. She had not voiced this concern, however, even to her own husband. Despite all their differences, Lucia was the rock that Mapp clung to. Life without her would be all the more dreary.

Similar telephone calls had been made to the Wyses, Bartletts, Diva and Quaint Irene and just before two, together with the Mapp-Flints, they met at the steps leading up to the imposing front door of Mallards House. They all knew that an 'important announcement' usually didn't refer to good news.

Mr. Wyse, wearing dark clothing like the others, took it upon himself to be the one to summon the household and gave a rather feeble tap on the door with his malacca cane. A collective mood of sadness hung about the air and little was said.

Grosvenor opened the door. She had been instructed to maintain a blank expression and to lead the visitors to the garden-room where a line of chairs had been arranged. Mapp noticed a signed photo of Noël Coward, placed upon the piano, reminding her of the fête just a few months ago and all the plotting that went with it. Happier times, indeed.

Georgie entered the room solemnly, perfectly groomed but looking nervous.

'Dear friends… my dear friends...' He coughed. 'As you know, Lucia has been at the very centre of our world for so many years. She has touched the lives of every single one of us.'

There was a collective sigh and a stifled sob from Irene.

'And she would not want us to be upset today, especially as,' Georgie paused deliberately, 'She is still with us.'

'Indeed, Pillson,' replied the Major, 'She'll always be with us.'

'In our hearts,' continued Mr. Wyse.

There was a louder sob from Irene and at this, Georgie could no longer keep up the pretence and a smile gradually appeared on his face.

'No, you all misunderstand me – Lucia really is still with us!'

There was an audible gasp as the side door opened and there stood Lucia, resplendent in a full-length red gown, wearing diamond earings and necklace which sparkled in the sunlight that was now streaming through the window.

'Dear friends, rumours of my death are an exaggeration – Mark Twain, I believe.'

She gave a broad smile and tossed her head a little, rather coquettishly.

'But we *really* thought you had died Lucia,' said Diva, with more than a hint of anger in her voice. 'Mr. Georgie, how can you be so cruel!'

'Please don't scold Georgie, Diva dear. He gave me his word that not one of you would be told of my recovery.'

'I did so want to let you know that Lucia was on the mend,' replied Georgie, 'but Lucia was adamant.'

In previous bouts of illness Lucia had always preferred to lock herself away from friends, rather than play the invalid. Being ill made Lucia feel vulnerable and a lack of control was anathema to her.

'Please forgive my sensibilities everyone, I am touched that everyone has been so concerned. I am delighted to be back, in full health and… your servant once more.'

At this, Algernon Wise bowed – perhaps lower than ever before.

'Diva, dear,' continued Mapp, 'Your over-active imagination again. We all had faith that dearest Lulu would pull through.'

Lucia looked Mapp straight in the eye.

'Black suits you so well Elizabeth.'

Moved to tears, Quaint Irene could no longer hold back and rushed to embrace Lucia.

'Darling Lucia, we desperately wanted to visit you at the hospital but there were strict instructions that no visitors were allowed.'

'Dear Irene, I have been at home for over a week now, regaining my strength and spirit and sorting out matters that have built up during my absence.'

Georgie was quite hopeless in the task of running a household and although Grosvenor and Foljamble had done their best to keep Mallards running smoothly, there were some functions that only Lucia herself could fulfill.

'At home for a week?' cried Irene. 'And you didn't say, Georgie?'

Georgie, now turning a shade of crimson, looked to the

floor. 'I was only following orders!'

'Mrs. Pillson, can I say, on behalf of us all, how delighted we are to welcome you back into the heart of Tilling,' and Mr. Wyse bowed, yet again.

'Three cheers for Lucia!' demanded Quaint Irene, leading the lively response.

The door opened and Grosvenor and Foljambe entered, carrying trays of Champagne and iced fruit cake. After the shock he had just had, the Major was in desperate need of some liquid sustenance.

'Do help yourselves, and perhaps you might care for a little Beethoven shortly?'

'Mrs. Pillson,' gasped Mr. Wyse, 'Are you up to it?'

'Dearest Mr. Wyse, Beethoven has been both my healer and faithfull companion since leaving the hospital!'

With stains of the *Moonlight Sonata* echoing into the kitchen, Grosvenor and Foljambe helped themselves to large glasses of Champagne.

'Don't you think that it was a bit cruel to make Mr. Georgie keep quiet about Mrs. Pillson's recovery?' asked Foljambe.

Grosvenor chuckled.

'Did you see the look on their faces when Mrs. Pillson entered the room. You'd have thought they'd seen a ghost!'

'At least my Cadman won't have to do any more midnight runs,' for Lucia had been brought back to Mallards in the early hours of the morning when the residents of Tilling were firmly tucked up in bed and fast asleep.

'And I can now look everybody in the eye without feeling

awkward. I'm certain that Ethel Withers knew that I wasn't telling the truth when she asked about Mrs. Pillson,' added Grosvenor, whose loyality had been severely tested in the last few weeks.

With Beethoven's final chord gently echoing around the room, Lucia sat motionless on the piano stool, her eyes firmly closed. Usually she would keep this position just long enough to emphasise the profundity of the music, but today she remained still for what seemed like an age. Susan Wyse was just about to ask Lucia whether she was feeling alright, when Lucia's eyes popped open and she slowly turned her head to her audience.

'I finer performance I have yet to hear, Mrs. Pillson,' said Mr. Wyse, visibly moved.

The Major – who had remained awake for the entire movement, agreed.

'A little more, perhaps?' he asked, much to the surprise of his wife.

'How you all work me!' replied Lucia and picked up an album of piano favourites. 'A little Schubert perhaps? Sight-reading of course!' and she checked the index for the C major waltz which she had first played over forty years earlier and, in preparation for guests arriving, had carefully practised just a few hours ago.

A few minutes later, Lucia and Georgie were saying their goodbyes to everyone. In complete contrast to their arrival at Mallards, the exit of their guests was marked by convivial joviality.

'Whit's fur ye'll no go by ye, Mistress Pillson!' said the

23

Padre, departing. A squeak from Evie confirming the sentiment.

'Well that seemed to go quite well, Lucia,' said Georgie as they returned to the garden-room.

'Elizabeth was very quiet, Georgie. I had expected a little more conversation from her.'

'I expect that she was rather taken aback by everything. She had obviously prepared herself for some bad news and…'

'Was rather put out that there wasn't any!' interrupted Lucia.

'Oh Lucia! I told you already that Mapp has been quite subdued recently. I expect she will perk up very soon.'

The next day, as the residents of Tilling did their marketing, there was much gossip as to the previous afternoon. Evie Bartlett bumped into Susan Wyse, who remarked that Lucia looked incredibly well for someone who had been so ill. The Vicar's wife had then visited Diva's tea-shop where Quaint Irene was finishing off a large mug of strong coffee.

'Looking a picture of health,' said Diva, as Evie took a chair opposite Miss Coles.

'Yes. Quite,' squeaked Evie.

'And pretty as a picture, I'd say,' added Irene. 'A period of illness can really emphasise the contours of a person's face. I must take my brushes round to Mallards.'

Quaint Irene's chair was quickly taken by Elizabeth who had just had a frustrating five minutes at Twistevant's. Her carefully prepared shopping list had been perused by Twistevant himself, with much shaking of the head.

'Haven't got that in, I'm afraid, Mrs. Mapp-Flint,' began Mr. Twistevant. 'I won't have any of those for at least two months – it's the wrong time of the year. And these,' pointing to the next item, 'I'm not stocking them any more but you can get them in Hastings.'

She was about to vent her frustration but managed to stop herself just in time. She did not wish to upset the chief purveyor of her jams and pickles.

'Will that be tea or coffee, Elizabeth?' asked Diva.

'A pot of tea Diva, dear and a fruit scone, please.'

'I'll ask Janet to boil a fresh kettle,' replied Diva. 'Any news?'

'Just seen Lucia,' replied Mapp, 'On her bicycle.'

'On her bicycle?'

'Yes, dear. Along Tilling High Street. Seemed as happy as Larry.'

'Well I never!' exclaimed Diva, 'And just off her deathbed too.'

'Indeed, dear one. You know that I am not one to judge, but I am beginning to suspect that dear Lulu wasn't quite as ill as we all thought.'

'It was just an insect bite, after all,' confirmed Evie.

'And who hasn't been bitten by some bug or other?' continued Mapp. 'Benjy was positively eaten alive by the ravenous creatures whilst in India and it did him no harm whatsoever.'

Diva and Evie gave each other a quizzical glance.

The Major himself had made his way to the Links for a spot of golf. Over the years, the number of strokes it took him to complete the course was gradually increasing and now his tally of birdies was easily outnumbered by his tally of bogies. However, the Major always viewed the sport as a means to an end and as he approached the nineteenth hole, the spring returned to his step.

'What can I get you Major?' asked the barman.

'Just the usual, please,' and he was handed a whisky and soda.

The first one usually went down in one gulp and the barman had already prepared a second.

'I hear that Mrs. Pillson is much better now,' said the barman. As a past Mayor of Tilling, Lucia's various comings and goings were still *res publica*.

'Remarkable woman!' replied the Major, 'Hardly believe she'd been ill. Breeding, you know,' and tipped the barman a knowing wink.

'One for the road, Major?' asked the barman, the Major having slugged his second whisky.

'Good chap! Put it on my tab will you?'

Chapter 3

A week had passed and Lucia had spent much of her time tending to her garden. The dahlias were still looking splendid. She had briefly entertained the thought of re-instigating her calisthenic regime but had decided that rigorous weeding was sufficient exercise alongside brisk walks and the occasional bike ride.

The clouds had lifted and the late autumn sunshine filtered through the trees, making the *giardino segreto* most inviting. Lucia sat in a wicker chair, a glass of fresh orange juice at her side. She had read an article in one of the hospital's magazines concerning the health benefits of various fruit and vegetable juices and following several experiments with carrots, red cabbage and beetroot had decided to stick with the traditional virgin fruit. She had written to both Daisy Quantock and Olga Bracely that morning. Daisy was now almost house-bound and eagerly awaited every letter sent by Lucia. Olga had just begun a six week appearance at the New York Metropolitan Opera in three different roles – singing Massanet, Verdi and, of course, Wagner. Before crossing the Atlantic and on hearing the distressing news about Lucia from Georgie she had insisted that she would cancel her performances in order to support Georgie. However, for once, Georgie had been even more insistant that Olga should fulfill her contract and not let her public down. 'It's what Lucia would want,' he had told her.

Grosvenor came with a tray carrying the morning post. Lucia always dealt with the day's correspondence. Even letters addressed to 'Mr. G. Pillson' came her way in the first instance, to be perused and then placed upon Georgie's desk later.

There were several good wishes cards, a couple of missives of a financial nature and a rather official-looking envelope with a large portcullis emblazoned on the front.
'I think that this could be very good news, Grosvenor!' exclaimed Lucia. 'Can you fetch Mr. Pillson immediately, please.'

Minutes later, Georgie appeared, slightly flustered as he been about to start the long and rather messy process of dying his remaining hair (so to match his toupée) and it's curtailment involved even more fuss and considerable distress.
'I do hope that this is important, Lucia,' he said, clearly annoyed.
'Please don't scold *ickle* Lucia,' she replied, 'I have *ickle* present for you!' and she passed him the letter.

Georgie stood motionless, letter in a slightly trembling hand. Lucia had a strong desire to grab the envelope herself and rip it open but knew that this was Georgie's moment. After a short pause he slowly and most carefully opened the envelope and began to read its contents.

'Good news, Georgie?' enquired Lucia.
'Very good news, in fact. I am to be given a knighthood in the New Year's Honours List for services to the arts.'

True to his word, David Webster, General Administrator of the Royal Opera House and guardian of a sizable amount of Pillson funds, had recently indicated that it would not be long before Georgie heard from Downing Street.

'But, I mustn't breathe a word to anyone.'

Georgie gave Lucia a worried look.

'Though I expect that I can tell you!'

Lucia took the letter and studied it closely. Georgie had not been given an ordinary knighthood – not that a knighthood was 'ordinary' in any sense, but a Baronetcy which Lucia understood to be a hereditary title. She pondered the latter point for a second or two and then dismissed it entirely.

'Sir George and Lady Pillson does have a rather elegant ring to it, Georgie,' said Lucia. 'I must remember to order some new stationary and contact the bank.'

'Not yet, Lucia!' exclaimed Georgie, now beginning to regret that Lucia was privy to the information so early on in the proceedings. 'We'll just have to wait and carry on exactly as normal – plain Mr. and Mrs. Pillson.'

A weak smile from Lucia was all the assurance he could hope for.

At Taormina, Quaint Irene was in the kitchen, arms in a sink full of hot soapy water, cleaning her brushes and palette alongside the empty plates and dishes that had built up during the last few days. She had recently been commissioned to paint a series of Biblical scenes for a church in Finchley and had taken advantage of the good weather to paint the ten small canvases in the garden. Lucy, her versatile six-foot maid, had modelled for Jezebel, the Virgin Mary and Cleopatra. Although the *real* Cleopatra was absent from the Bible, there was a mention of a Cleopatra in the First Book of Maccabees, and that was good enough for Irene.

There was a knock on the door. As Lucy was out on an errand, Irene went to answer it.

'Well, Mapp! What a lovely surprise! Come to get your portrait updated? I can add a few more lines.'

'How you tease, Quaint one!' replied Mapp who was quite used to Irene's wicked sense of humour.

'I was wondering whether you would be kind enough to donate one of your pictures for the charity auction to raise money for the Tilling Hospital? As a former Mayoress, I still try to keep an interest in all matters civic.' Whilst the hospital was now part of the National Health Service, many of the services it provided were still funded by private donations and bequests.

'A finger in all the pies I'd say, Mapp! I'll dig something out and call round later.'

'Thank you, dear one. Au reservoir!' trilled Mapp – mission accomplished.

Next, she made her way to Wasters where Diva Plaistow sat alone, waiting for a customer to visit her tea-shop. Demand was usually sporadic during the week, though a sunny weekend could be bring in the crowds – not because her tea-shop was particularly renowned but, more the case, it was the *only* tea-shop in Tilling.

'A nice pot of tea, Diva dear and a slice of Victoria sponge, please.'

Pleased to receive a paying guest, Diva went to the kitchen, instructing Janet who was baking a batch of cheese straws, to make up a tray for two.

Diva returned, proudly carrying a plate full of coconut macaroons.

'New addition, Mapp,' she explained. 'Wanted to wait until Lucia had got better.'

'Really dear? Well I am sure that she will be honoured to know that the introduction of a macaroon to the menu was delayed due to her unfortunate absence.'

Diva wasn't sure whether Mapp's comment was laced with a little sarcasm.

'Cherry?' asked Diva

The macaroons were adorned with either a bright red glacé cherry or a little piece of candied peel.

'Am I testing them, Diva, or paying for them?

'Just want an opinion, Elizabeth. I made the cherry ones and Janet made the others.'

'Then, why don't I try both?' and she picked the two largest macaroons off the plate.

Janet arrived with the tea and served both Mapp and Diva. A little plate of freshly baked cheese straws looked very tempting.

'Quaint Irene has kindly agreed to give one of her pictures for the Hospital auction,' informed Mapp, 'Though I hope it's a suitable one.'

Although Quaint Irene had a notorious reputation for depicting controversial subjects in her paintings, this had

31

lifted her profile immensely in the art world. Since painting *The Birth of Venus* comically featuring both Mapp and Benjy, which had been exhibited at the Royal Academy, original Coles were now sought after, fetching increasingly higher prices. Even the harshest of critics acknowledged her passion, referring to her 'admirable eccentricity'.

'Lots of naked flesh, probably,' pondered Diva, remembering the time, many years ago, when she had shocked the late Mr. Plaistow by agreeing to be one of Irene's first ever life models.

'Hopefully not dear. Now, I might have room one one little cheese straw,' and she picked up a handful.

Susan Wise looked lovingly at her MBE medal, which she kept close at hand in a little ivory box on top of the mahogany bookshelf. Occasionally she would wear it around the house as she busied herself with her daily duties and would purposely walk past the large mirror in the hall, checking the positioning of the insignia.

Algernon Wise was talking to his sister, Amelia, the Contessa di Faraglione, on the telephone. She had arrived in London the previous day and would be visiting her brother the next. Used to the constant sunshine of Capri, where even in the winter months the temperature remained relatively warm, the Contessa found the unpredictable British weather rather annoying. In fact, she found lots of things annoying. In turn, Susan was obliged to forgo her objections to smoking in the house when Amelia made her visits.

Replacing the telephone receiver, Mr. Wyse returned to his wife.

'Dear Amelia will be coming to stay with us tomorrow.'

Susan gave the expected smile and was just about to ask whether it was for one night only when her husband continued.

'Sadly, just the single night.'

Susan forced a look of disappointment.

Well-connected, the Contessa had already made arrangements to visit the Earl of Kimberley in Norfolk, for most of her brief stay. She had originally met him in Switzerland, whilst watching the famous Cresta Run.

'Perhaps we can invite the Pillsons to join us for dinner, Susan?'

'Delightful, Algernon!'

Lucia's encounters with the Contessa had always been rather tense affairs. This situation was due, in large part, to the fact that Lucia's command of the Italian language was fairly rudimentary despite professing to be a fluent speaker of *la bella lingua*. Mapp had suspected as much but had failed to unmask Lucia, despite several attempts.

Therefore Lucia was reluctant to give an immediate acceptance to the invitation when Mr. Wyse telephoned later that day.

'The Contessa will be most upset if she can't meet you, Mrs. Pillson. And how I love to hear the world's most enchanting language being spoken *proprio come un italiano*!'

Lucia shuddered and promised to ring Mr. Wyse back once she had consulted with Georgie.

33

Georgie, having spent most evenings at Mallards for seemingly ages, was keen to accept the invitation, knowing full well why Lucia was dithering.

'At least Mapp won't be there, Lucia. She won't be able to goad. We'll just steer clear of anything to do with Italy. Or you could lose your voice?'

'Not again, Georgie!' she sighed.

Georgie suddenly perked up.

'I have an idea, Lucia. Let's call it Plan A.'

'It needs to be foolproof, Georgie.'

'Well, if Plan A fails, we've still got twenty-five letters left!'

Lucia did not appreciate Georgie's attempt at humour in the slightest.

Chapter 4

Lucia had her misgivings. Some plans seemed well-conceived, some mischievous and some plain silly. In this case, and on reflection, the latter applied and she wished she had not let Georgie talk her into accepting the invitation and convince her that his plan would work. She spent the next day fussing around, moving papers from one draw to another, then back again, checking the provisions in the kitchen, even though Grosvenor had provided her with a full inventory only the previous week and undertaking various other tasks of little or no importance.

Grosvenor was now serving afternoon tea – a tradition that was still popular in the upper echelons of Tilling society. Lucia looked at the plate of fish paste sandwiches with some disdain. Fish paste was not her favourite sandwich filling but was readily obtainable, wholesome and nutritious. During the War, she recalled, half of the population had survived on fish paste alone. And she, herself, had suffered the consequences of a fish-only diet for several months many years ago. At least Grosvenor had supplied several slices of lemon Madeira cake, a particular favourite of hers, to soften the blow.

After eating his allocation of sandwiches, several of Lucia's and two slices of cake, Georgie spoke.
'Cadman will take us to Starling Cottage at six thirty.'
Lucia, who was now browsing an Italian dictionary, looked up.

'And put that thing away, Lucia! Remember our plan!'

'Your plan, Georgie, I believe,' and she put the book down on the arm of the sofa and sighed, rather petulantly. 'Perhaps we should cancel, Georgie. My throat *is* feeling a little sore.'

'Nonsense, Lucia! Stop sulking and pull yourself together!'

Georgie rarely admonished Lucia but, on the odd occasion, would vent his anger out loud. When this occurred, Lucia would, for a short while at least, play the obedient wife. She moved off the sofa and went upstairs to soak in a hot bath, in which she placed a generous measure of verbena bath salts. Georgie hoped that a hot soak would prove beneficial and improve her demeanor.

An hour later, Lucia reappeared in the garden-room, looking most elegant in a green rayon dress, a set of seed pearls around her neck. A platinum diamond-set hair grip sparkled in the fading sunlight.

'That's better, Lucia,' said Georgie, encouragingly. 'Let's make the most of the evening. Mr. Wyse usually has one or two interesting stories and the Contessa…'

'Likes the sound of her own voice, Georgie!'

'Hopefully, neither of us will be able to get a word in edgeways!'

They both laughed as they heard the Rolls draw up outside the front door.

Cadman had just moved into second gear when the Rolls arrived in Porpoise Street and the journey came to an end. He opened the doors for Lucia and Georgie and waited in the car until they had been admitted into Starling Cottage. He planned to drive straight on to Broad Oak and open up the throttle. There was a very good public house on the way and he planned to stop there for a pint of beer, or perhaps two.

'Dear Mr. and Mrs. Pillson, so delighted to welcome you to Starling Cottage. My sister, the Contessa di Faraglione and my dear wife, Susan, await you in the drawing room.' Mr Wyse bowed in turn to both Georgie and Lucia.
'So looking forward to seeing the Contessa again,' replied Lucia.
'And to converse *Italiano*. It will be *molto agréable*! A sweet sherry?' asked Mr. Wyse, 'Or perhaps a glass of *Marsala Vergine Stravecchio* that dear Amelia has brought with her?'

The Contessa and Susan were sat with their glasses on two large upholstered armchairs, placed on either side of the fireplace, in which a solitary log was burning, providing some ambience but little heat. Susan's MBE was in full view, surrounded by a little feather arrangement. Lucia and Georgie sat down opposite them on a cottage-style sofa that not only looked uncomfortable but *was* uncomfortable – extremely so, thought Georgie, who suffered from occasional lumbago. Mr Wyse faced them, his back towards the fire.

'Tilling is indeed blessed to have you back, Mrs. Pillson. I have informed my sister, Amelia, of your unfortunate circumstances.'
'It must have been dreadful!' said the Contessa. 'I

37

absolutely detest hospitals. And doctors! And most nurses seem to fuss around doing little of any consequence.'

'Oh, Lucia had a most wonderful doctor,' replied Georgie. 'He prescribed penicillin which undoubtedly saved her life.'

'Yes, they've just started to use that in Italy,' continued the Contessa. 'A dear friend's husband had three fingers bitten off by their pet Doberman last March. He might have lost his whole arm but for penicillin. A real tragedy – they had to have the dog put down!'

Susan entertained a brief thought that a Doberman would not dare bite the Contessa.

'And are there any side effects associated with this drug?' enquired Susan.

Georgie gave Lucia a quick glance. Was providence at play?

'We were given a list by the doctor,' continued Lucia. 'A rather long list, I'm afraid. But, so far, I seem to have avoided the worst of them. I still have my appetite and the headaches have eased. I can't really recall what else I should be suffering!'

'There's another,' said Georgie.

'Another what?' asked Mr. Wyse.

'Another side effect. Memory loss,' replied Georgie. 'Dr. Kendrick did tell us that after taking penicillin, some patients can suffer acute memory loss.'

'I don't remember him saying that, Georgie.'

'Well, there you are then!'

'Indeed!' confirmed Mr. Wyse. 'A little more sherry?'

The Contessa was warming up now and began to tell everybody about her recent trip to Africa. She had stayed in Salisbury, Southern Rhodesia, the guest of a tobacco magnate and therefore had no qualms about smoking in the guest bedroom. She had been taken out on safari and had encountered what seemed like a friendly lioness with her two small cubs.

'I have always been quite partial to cats and the driver assured me that it would be quite safe to step off the vehicle and move closer to the lion cubs,' continued the Contessa.

'That sounds rather dangerous,' said Georgie. 'I believe that the mothers are very protective of their young.'

'A massive understatement, Mr. Pillson,' added Mr. Wyse. 'Dear Amelia was almost mauled to death.'

'How dreadful!' exclaimed Lucia, examining the Contessa a little more closely. 'You appear to be unscathed. Were you just slightly mauled?'

'Fortuitously, Amelia's companion fired off a shot to scare the beast away and she was able to return to the vehicle, blemish free,' explained Mr. Wyse.

'It must have been a shock, Amelia,' sympathised Susan.

'Just a few stiff brandies needed. By the way, Algernon, can you top up my glass?' and she thrust it forward, awaiting the refill.

Dinner was substantial but, in Lucia's opinion, lacked flair. A game terrine was followed by a shoulder of pork accompanied by root vegetables and a slightly undercooked potato gratin, with *Torta della Nonna*, baked in tribute to the Contessa, for dessert. More custard pie than *Torta*, the absence of cream did the dish no favours. Surprisingly, throughout the meal, the Contessa spoke not one word of Italian. Lucia noticed that, when eating, she took rather large mouthfuls – an obvious reason for the preclusion of vigorous conversation. Added to that the pork was a little tough and needed rigorous chewing.

Afterwards, Mr. Wyse withdrew to his study to return with a small book with a bright red leather cover.
'Just arrived last week. A love token from dear Susan,' and he turned his head meaningfully towards his wife. 'A new volume of poems by Ungaretti – *La Terra Promessa*. It would be an honour to hear one or two spoken out loud,' and he bowed to the Contessa and Lucia, passing the book to his sister.

The Contessa positioned her monocle and opened up the book, scanned the index and began reading. Not a great patron of the arts, her delivery lacked any sense of emotion as she spoke in a dreary monotone. Georgie thought that she could be reading absolutely anything – instuctions to fit the bag on the Hoover, for example, or the ingrediants for a Christmas cake, but her brother, smiling broadly, seemed to be enjoying the rendition.

'*Bel canto*, Amelia!' cheered Mr. Wyse. Not quite the right expression but near enough. 'Now, Mrs. Pillson, a little Ungaretti from you?'
The Contessa passed Lucia the book. She mentally crossed her fingers as she opened it.

There was a long pause as she stared blankly at the pages.

'Is everything alright, Lucia?' asked Georgie.

'How strange, Georgie. I don't recognise any of the words!'

'What do you mean, Lucia?'

'It's as if I am looking at a foreign language,' which, indeed, she was.

'How odd,' said Mr. Wyse. 'Has it lost all meaning? Amelia, please say something to Mrs. Pillson in Italian.'

'*Che non men che saver, dubbiar m'aggrata*,' responded the Contessa. 'Dante, I believe.'

Lucia blank expression remained and she shook her head desolately.

There was another awkward pause. Then suddenly, Susan spoke up, just beating Georgie who was about to utter the same conclusion.

'It must be the penicillin, Algernon. Mr. Pillson said earlier that acute memory loss was a possible side effect. It's quite obvious that Mrs. Pillson has forgotten how to speak Italian.'

'How curious!' replied Mr. Wyse.

'Unique, I'd say,' added the Contessa, who had her own suspicions about Lucia's proficiency in Italian, though this was of little concern to her.

'We must inform Dr. Kendrick, Georgie,' said Lucia. 'I might be able to make a contribution to medical science.'

'How exciting!' remarked Susan, 'Italian amnesia!'

Lucia could now relax, knowing that Georgie's plan had worked. To the amusement of both Lucia and Georgie,

Mr. Wyse later professed to seeing an article about the condition in the *John Bull* magazine. Maybe it *was* a genuine side-effect of the drug after all but Lucia did not care in the slightest.

The Contessa returned to the armchair by the side of the fire, a fresh glass of the *Marsala* in her hand.

'Do tell me about about Noël Coward's visit to Mallards, Mrs. Pillson, I'm such a fan. He's a regular visitor to Capri in the summer months.'

'Dearest Noël,' replied Lucia, 'Such a good friend. He sent so many cards and flowers to the hospital.'

Georgie recalled just a single missive.

'Once his numerous commitments in London had been fulfilled, he couldn't wait to visit Tilling and be the Guest of Honour at our little fête. Poor Elizabeth Mapp-Flint failed to recognise him – thought that he was some kind of look-alike!'

'How embarrassing!' exclaimed the Contessa.

'More for her, I think. Noël was quite amused,' replied Lucia.

'And he delighted us all with a few of his songs,' chipped in Mr. Wyse. 'Such a wit!'

'Humour to be savoured, Mr. Wyse – just like caviar,' pronounced Lucia. 'He has promised that he will pay another visit shortly.'

'Really?' wondered Georgie.

'In fact, he was interested in discussing a few ideas I had for a new play. We have such a lot in common!'

'Really?' wondered Georgie again, musing that he himself probably had more in common with Noël Coward than his wife.

'A new play sounds very exciting,' continued Susan. 'Are you at liberty to discuss the content?'

Lucia, thinking on her feet, began to regurgitate a truncated version of the plot of *Love in a Cold Climate* which she guessed (correctly) no one had yet read.

'Just an outline, of course. I'll leave the actual dialogue to Noël himself. I wouldn't dare suggest that I write the whole thing myself.'

'Dear Mrs. Pillson, might I suggest that you do! You mustn't be a coward!' said Mr. Wyse.

'Coward?' said Georgie, slighty bemused.

'Coward!' shrieked the Contessa. 'Very good Algernon!'

Mr. Wyse bowed, a self-congratulatory grin reinforcing the notion that his own wit was almost as sharp as the great man himself.

Chapter 5

Lucia had always had money. Before marriage to her dear Pepino she had well-off parents to support her. Pepino himself had earned a handsome salary and on his death had amassed enough wealth to keep Lucia in comfortable circumstances for the rest of her life. However, it was Lucia herself who had generated the lion's share of her fortune, a lucky investment in (and subsequent quick exit from) Siriami shares had started the ball rolling. Her dalliance with the stock market, either by design or sheer good fortune, had reaped rich rewards and when she had passed on the responsibility of managing her large portfolio to her stockbroker, things had improved even further. Having made shrewd investments in the States, the rise of the dollar in the late 1940s had considerably swelled the coffers.

By way of contrast, Mapp's fortunes were continuing their slow downward spiral. What Mapp could save on the weekly provisions by buying a cheaper cut of meat or managing with just two Fry's Peppermint Creme bars per week, Benjy could easily spend at the nineteenth hole. Whilst others bemoaned the continuation of rationing, Mapp was grateful that the strict regime remained.

Lucia was sat at her desk, her pince-nez perched precariously on the end of her nose. In front of her lay pages and pages of figures and calculations. Although she enjoyed the rigours of financial management, the money itself had always been of secondary importance – until now.

Ever since her 'near death' experience, Lucia had pondered the thought of her dying and leaving a massive fortune in flux. On marrying Georgie, she had, of course, altered her Will in his favour but how would he cope with all that money if she wasn't there to advise him? What would he spend it on and, more worryingly, who might wish to influence him? She admired Olga in many ways but considered her a spendthrift.

Georgie brushed past Lucia. He had been in a particularly good mood all morning since finding a sovereign in the inside pocket of an old coat that he was about to give to the Padre for the upcoming Church jumble sale, and was whistling *Non più andrai* from Mozart's *Marriage of Figaro*. He had happily passed on the coat but had put the coin in a jar in his dressing room.

He stopped whistling and looked over Lucia's shoulder, playfully exclaiming 'What a lot of noughts Lucia!'
Like his wife, Georgie never discussed money – he didn't need to as there appeared to be a limitless supply.
'Yes,' replied Lucia, 'Too many in fact. I have decided that I must divest a sizable proportion of my funds… for the good of the people, Georgie.'
'What people?' asked Georgie, rather incredulously.
'Those who do not share our good fortunes, Georgie. And remember the wise words of Isaiah 'It is easier for a camel to pass through the eye of a needle than for a rich man to enter the kingdom of heaven,' Georgie.'

Georgie was used to Lucia's occasional Biblical misquotations and did not correct her.

'I intend to set up a Charitable Trust, Georgie, and pay the interest I receive from all my investments into it. Of course, I would transfer a lump sum into the Trust to begin with – to get the ball rolling.'

'And then?'

'I would ask for written bids for funding of good works from the residents of Tilling. There are so many needy people out there who are desperate for help. If I can bring a smile to some of those poor unfortunate faces, then I shall be happy.'

'And who would consider these bids?' asked Georgie, 'You need to have a Board of Trustees, presumably?'

Lucia had not considered this, thinking that her own personal decision would suffice – after all, it was her own money.

'You can't dole out money to all and sundry, Lucia,' continued Georgie.

'Of course, Georgie and I was just about to ask you whether you would be kind enough to join the Board?' she replied with as much conviction as she could muster.

'I would be delighted, Lucia!' replied Georgie, slightly taken aback. 'Perhaps I should ask the Padre to join? Church and all that.'

Lucia bit her lip. Georgie had only just been invited to join the Board and he was already making decisions which were, undoubtedly, hers to make.

'We will discuss appointments later, Georgie. Now, how about a little *musica* to celebrate the launch of the Trust?' and Lucia moved to the piano where a volume of

Delibes' 'Greatest Melodies' arranged for piano duet stood on the music rest.

'Perhaps the *Flower Duet*, Georgie?'

'Oh, yes please! I'll sit on the left, Lucia, the *primo* part looks far too difficult!'

'Well, I'll give it my best shot,' replied Lucia who had already played the music through on several occasions, unbeknown to Georgie.

'*Uno, due, tres…*'

Mapp had emptied her jar of shillings out onto the kitchen table and was counting the last few, stacking them into neat piles. Normally she would wait for the jar to become full before adding up the contents and taking them to the bank. However, several bills had appeared all at once and every shilling counted. The Major entered the kitchen.

'Six pounds, nine shillings, Benjy. That's enough to pay the Water Board and settle the coal bill.'

'Well done Liz-girl!' replied the Major, who genuinely admired his wife's ability to forgo life's little luxuries in order to balance the books. The shilling jar had come to their rescue yet again. The Major felt a pang of guilt – his occasional habit of secretly raiding the jar was becoming less 'occasional' each month. Bar bills did not pay themselves.

'Why don't we walk into Tilling and visit Diva's tea-shop for a treat?' suggested the Major.

Mapp was a frequent visitor to Diva's front parlour but

joint visits were rare. Seizing the opportunity to accompany her husband, she replied enthusiastically.

'I suppose we *could* spend a few shillings. Two of Diva's delicious eighteen penny teas,' and she pocketed a handful of coins.

'Perhaps another coconut macaroon, Mrs. Plaistow?' asked the Major, holding out his plate, Oliver-like.

'You've already had three, Benjy!' his wife replied, a mouth full of egg sandwich.'

'I'm sure that Janet has a few more spare, Major. I'll just go and check,' and Diva returned to the kitchen.

In conversation, Diva had told Mapp that Lucia was suffering from Italian amnesia. Susan Wyse had imparted the information whilst queuing at the butcher's shop that very morning. From Diva's description, it was not entirely certain whether Lucia had simply forgotten how to speak the language or whether Italian amnesia was a *bona fide* medical condition. Mapp's intuition told her that the whole thing was as fishy as Diva's sardine tartlets.

Chapter 6

Mapp looked out of the window. A solitary blackbird was attempting to extricate a rather large worm from the front lawn. Mapp watched it for a good few minutes as it continued its struggle, tugging the helpless worm inch by inch from its underground lair. Suddenly the bird took flight, the fruits of its labours dangling from its beak.

Darkened skies indicated the likelihood of a heavy downpour. The weather had been rather unsettled recently and the tides had been worryingly high the last couple of nights. Not one to be put off by a spot of rain, the Major had already left Grebe for an early morning round of golf. Mapp intended to pay a visit to her capacious attic room, a chore that she had been putting off for several weeks.

When the Mapp-Flints had moved from Mallards to Grebe, as well as selling some large items of furniture to Lucia (at a knock down price Mapp recalled), many other possessions had been stored in the attic at Grebe. Amongst the collective junk, there were numerous boxes of books, several bone china dinner and tea sets (inevitably none were complete), various items of bed linen, curtains and towels, a whole gallery of pictures of dubious quality stacked in a corner and an oak chest full of oddments inherited from her Aunt Caroline. It was Mapp's intention to root out some of these odds and ends and take them to an antique shop in nearby Winchelsea, should they be of sufficient quality or possible value. A little extra income would be most welcome.

Mapp eventually found the pole that opened the attic hatch – the Major had previously used it to retrieve a handkerchief that had fallen behind the sofa, and she tugged furiously on the sectioned ladder which finally fell into place, its rickity steps rather uninviting. Mapp slowly ascended, feeling for the light switch near the top of the steps. She had made this journey many times before but always seemed to misjudge the distance between the ladder and the switch as she lunged into the blackness, perched precariously on the top rung. However, today, there were no such problems and the roof space was soon lit by a single forty watt bulb.

A heavy layer of dust covered most of the boxes, giant cobwebs adding to the arcane setting. Unmistakable evidence of mice could be seen on the bare wooden floorboards as well as a half-decayed crow that must have entered the attic via a broken slate on the roof and had sadly failed to find an exit.

The chest was in the far corner of the attic, large and imposing with carved sides and a substantial brass lock, now broken. As a child, Mapp remembered visiting her beloved Aunt, being given a shiny, golden key and being allowed to search in the chest for some object of amusement. Containing her Aunt's own childhood toys, games and dolls, the young Elizabeth would spend many happy hours playing in her own make-believe world.

Now, so many years later, a couple of the dolls were still in the chest, their dresses grubby and faded, their porcelain heads still showing evidence of the rouge and lipstick that Mapp had once applied to them, much to her Aunt's annoyance. Mapp took one of them out and hugged it. Happy childhood memories came flooding back as well as a few less pleasant ones as she recalled her phantom pregnancy, the visible sign of which Lucia had termed a 'wind egg'.

Mapp lifted out the contents of the chest one by one. A Victorian tortoiseshell needle case looked promising, its collection of needles still intact, as did a lined mahogany tea caddy. Next, Mapp found a pair of silver candlesticks which she had long forgotten about. On closer inspection, and to Mapp's disappointment, the letters EPNS were clearly visible on the base. Finding some hallmarked silver spoons and a pair of ornate sugar tongs, her mood lifted a little.

Moving to where a stack of pictures lay, there was an ominous creak and Mapp failed to notice a large split that had appeared in the wooden floor. As she took another step, there was a loud crack as the floor gave way and Mapp fell through the sizable hole, saved from completely falling through by her ample bust.

It all happened so quickly that Mapp had no time to scream. Although in a state of shock, she wasn't hurt and could move both her legs as they dangled from her bedroom ceiling, broken timbers scattered on her bed below. The hole held her tight and despite several attempts to wriggle free, she remained trapped. It was no use calling for Withers as she had the morning off and was visiting her aunt in Tunbridge Wells. Hopefully, Benjy would not be too long.

Having enjoyed the hospitality of the nineteenth hole, the Major had taken a leisurely stroll back from the Links to Grebe, taking advantage of a public bench, halfway into his journey, dozing for ten minutes or so. When he eventually arrived back, he immediately made his way to his favourite armchair, kicked off his shoes and called Withers.
'Quai hai!' boomed the Major.
Withers was not due back until mid-afternoon and it took a minute or so for Benjy to register that she was not about. Thinking that Elizabeth must be out too, and taking advantage of the situation, he poured himself a generous measure of whisky (no soda) and switched on the radio.

Any sounds that he might have heard from Mapp, her legs dangling from the ceiling just one floor above, were masked by the sound of the Joe Loss Orchestra playing on the Light Programme.

Nine times out of ten, the major would have fallen asleep at this point but today he was feeling rather peckish. He got up and made his way to the kitchen in order to make himself a sandwich. He opened up the cupboard where Mapp stored her jams and pickles and reached for the back, retrieving a jar of brilliant-red raspberry jam. Surely she wouldn't notice if he 'borrowed' just a sliver of the tasty conserve to spread on his bread and butter?

Delicious! Elizabeth Mapp-Flint was certainly the best jam-maker in Tilling! By comparison, Diva's jam, served either on buttered toast or surmounting her plump fruit scones, was rather too sweet, excess sugar compensating for a lack of fruit.

As the Major returned to his whisky, he heard a noise coming from upstairs. In her sporadic struggle, Mapp had dislodged a further section of ceiling plaster which had crashed down onto her dressing table, knocking over several bottles of scent, shampoo and digestion tonic. The Major, thinking that there might be burglars at large, quickly grabbed a nearby umbrella – just in case he needed to give anyone a whack, and gingerly made his way up the stairs. As he approached the top, he saw that the attic-room was open and began to ascend the steps.

'Benjy! Benjy! Is that you?' asked a rather panicked voice from above.
'Elizabeth?'
'I'm stuck, Benjy! Where have you been?'
The Major, rather unsteadily, stepped off the ladder and entered the attic. There was Mapp, only the top third of her visible, looking strained and teary-eyed.

'What on earth happened, Liz-girl?' asked the Major in his most comforting voice.
'The floor gave way and I've been stuck here for hours!' wailed Mapp. 'Come and get me out!'
The Major grabbed Mapp's arms and pulled with all his

53

might but she would not move.

''Pull harder, Benjy!' ordered Mapp as the Major made another failed attempt to dislodge her. He looked through a gap in the floorboards.

'Perhaps it would be easier if I push you down – you'll land on the bed.'

'No!' screamed Mapp as the Major placed both his hands on the top of her head and was about to push. 'Just call the Fire Brigade, Benjy. Quick!'

'Are you sure?'

'Yes, Benjy. Phone 999!'

It had been some years since he had phoned the emergency number and after giving his name, address and confirming that the incident was indeed an emergency, he rang off. Thus the fire crew that arrived twenty minutes later had no idea as to the exact nature of their rescue, though a lack of smoke clearly indicated that there was no fire.

Benjy was waiting for them by the front door.

'It's my wife. She's fallen through the floor in the attic and is stuck. Can't budge her myself.'

The fire officer went upstairs, looked in the bedroom where two thirds of Mapp was residing and then moved up to the attic itself.

'Now don't you worry ma'am,' said the officer, reassuringly, 'We'll soon have you out.'

He was soon joined by two other members of the crew and the three of them attempted to pull Mapp out of the hole. All seemed to be going well until Mapp let out a piercing scream as a jagged piece of wood cut into the top of her left leg. Not wishing to inflict any more pain, the firemen stopped the procedure and began to discuss alternatives.

There were a few nods and some shakings of heads and finally the senior fire officer spoke.
'We are going to push you through the hole, Mrs. Mapp-Flint and, don't worry, we'll catch you below!'
'Be careful,' said the Major, who was now becoming a little concerned.

The two junior officers positioned themselves directly underneath Mapp, prepared for a substantial weight to drop. As the senior officer pushed, Mapp's legs flailed about, the ceiling creaked and a further large crack appeared. Suddenly, there was a very loud sound of timbers splitting and the whole ceiling gave way. Wood and plaster fell at great speed, together with Mapp towards the bedroom floor. In a split second it was all over, everyone covered in dust and debris. The two fireman felt that they had earned their day's wages as they cradled a dazed Elizabeth Mapp-Flint in their arms.

'Good show, chaps!' said the Major as the firemen carried Mapp downstairs and placed her on the settee. 'Can I offer you a drink?'
'Not whilst we're on duty, sir. But your wife could do with one. And that cut could do with a plaster, sir.'
'Ah, yes! A brandy, I think,' and the Major poured Elizabeth half a tumbler of Martell Fine Cognac – only to be consumed to celebrate very special occasions or for

medicinal purposes and emergencies. Then he went into the kitchen to find the First Aid kit which contained a pack of Band-Aid sticking plasters. Returning with the largest available size, he carefully applied it to his wife's wound.

'Thank you, Benjy,' said Mapp, wearily, and she took another sip of the brandy. 'And thank you gentlemen,' addressing the three firemen.
'All in a day's work, ma'am,' and they made their way back to the fire engine.
'Bit of a weight, that one,' giggled the youngest fireman as they drove back to the station.

Brandy all finished, Mapp was on the verge of sleep, the pain in her leg dissipating as the drink took hold. She smiled dreamily at Benjy and closed her eyes. A few minutes later, a gentle snoring could be heard from the sofa.

Withers returned soon afterwards.
'Is everything all right, Major,' she asked, noticing a rather dusty Mapp asleep on the sofa, the empty brandy glass by her side.
'Just a spot of bother, Withers. Mrs. Mapp-Flint has had a slight accident. The bedroom will need a bit of a tidy up.'
'Yes, sir. I'll see to that right away.'
As she entered the bedroom, Wither's scream was almost as loud as that of her employer!

The following week, Mapp received a whole host of visitors as news of her accident and dramatic rescue spread. The sticking plaster had been replaced by an over-sized surgical bandage and her story had been further embellished with each visit.

'If the fire brigade had arrived any later then this leg would have had to be amputated, Diva!'

'Gosh Elizabeth! You're so brave! Does it hurt?

'As you know, Godiva, dear, I'm not one to complain,' and she grimaced purposefully as she rubbed the bandage. 'I'm sure that I will be up and about very soon. Thank goodness I have my dear Benjy-boy to comfort me.'

'Yes, it must be nice to have a man around the house,' replied Diva, whistfully, as faded memories of Mr. Plaistow briefly returned.

Lucia and Georgie called on the Mapp-Flints towards the end of the week. Georgie carried a small posy of flowers, hand-picked from the garden, which he had secured with a red silk ribbon. Lucia brought a tin of homemade chocolate biscuits, freshly baked. As they approached Grebe in the Rolls, Lucia was certain that she could see Mapp staring out from one of the bedroom windows and she was equally sure that she could hear someone furiously running down the stairs as Georgie knocked on the front door, which was answered by the Major.

'Ah, Mr. and Mrs. Pillson! Do come in. Elizabeth is just in here,' and the Major showed them to where Mapp was lying on the sofa, apparently asleep.

'You musn't wake her on our account, Major,' said Lucia. 'I expect that dear Elizabeth is still very frail and needs all the rest she can get.'

At this, Mapp yawned dramatically and opened her eyes. Seeing Lucia and Georgie, a feigned look of surprise appeared on her face. Adding to the deception, she made an attempt to raise herself from the sofa but failed miserably.

'Please don't exert yourself, Elizabeth. I know from bitter experience that illness and overexertion feed from each other.'

'Yes, dear,' replied Mapp, not quite sure what Lucia had meant.

'Benjy, ask Withers to bring a pot of tea, will you?'

'And I have brought some delicious biscuits, Elizabeth,' said Lucia as she opened the tin, releasing the pungent smell of dark chocolate.

In the Mapp-Flint household, chocolate biscuits were items of extreme luxury, so the beaming smile that now appeared on Mapp's face was entirely genuine. As the Mapp-Flints and the Pillsons finished their tea and biscuits, small talk exhausted, Lucia and Georgie returned to Cadman and the Rolls.

'How is Mrs. Mapp-Flint, ma'am,' enquired Cadman.

'On top form, Cadman! On top form!'

Chapter 7

It was the day of the Investiture. Georgie had dined lightly the previous evening and although he had retired early, he had had little sleep. The butterflies in his stomach had beaten their delicate wings most furiously. He was now feeling rather light-headed and somewhat wobbly on the feet.

There was a knock on Georgie's bedroom door.

'Georgie, are you awake?'

Lucia had risen at five, breakfasted at six and was now, at precisely seven o' clock, fully dressed in a powder-blue silk gown.

'Yes,' answered Georgie feebly, behind closed doors, 'But I'm feeling rather nervous.'

'Nervous?' replied Lucia, 'Why on earth should you be nervous, Georgie? All you have to do is stand there. You're not making a speech!'

'Oh I know that Lucia, but it's all the pomp and circumstance beforehand. I'm sure that once it's all over, I shall be fine.'

'Georgino mio! Have you not been Drake to my Elizabeth? Have not I myself anointed your shoulders?'

'Well, yes,' answered Georgie.

'Then you are fully prepared for the task in hand!'

Lucia moved aside as Foljambe made her way to Georgie's door. As usual, she knocked politely but entered immediately without any instruction. She heard Foljambe reassure Georgie that everything was going to be fine and that they would both have a wonderful day.

Lucia then went back downstairs to pack her handbag.

By the time he had got dressed - top hat and tails of course, Georgie's queasy disposition was beginning to fade. Foljambe was absolutely right! This was going to be a splendid day!

Cadman knocked on the front door of Mallards, signalling that the beautifully polished Rolls-Royce was ready. He gave a quick nod of the head as Lucia, Georgie and Foljambe stepped outside. Nodoubt a more sincere and visible nod would be needed for Sir George and Lady Pillson. Lucia quickly made her way to the front seat, leaving Georgie and Foljambe to sit in the back.

'Cadman!' exclaimed Lucia, cheerfully, 'Take us to the Palace!'

'Right you are ma'am,' replied Cadman, also in buoyant mood, as the car purred into action.

A distance of some eighty miles or so, Cadman's steady but sure driving got them to their destination in just under two hours. During the journey Georgie had been reading *Notes for Knights*, a handy pamphlet of do's and don'ts, supplied by the Investiture Committee. Amongst other things, it advised those attending the ceremony to refrain from blowing their noses, sucking peppermints and 'fawning'. Lucia had brought with her a well-thumbed copy of Dante's *Inferno*, but it had remained unread and Foljambe had fallen to sleep – gentle snores and the occasional snort masked by the sound of the engine.

The Investiture was due to commence at eleven thirty,

followed by a lunchtime reception in the grounds of Buckingham Palace. Cadman parked near The Mall, allowing Lucia, Georgie and Foljambe to walk leisurely through St. James's Park and on to the Palace. On arrival, they were whisked off to the smaller of the waiting rooms – the Green Drawing Room which was reserved for CBEs, Knights and above with those receiving the lower orders sent to the Picture Gallery. A softly-spoken gentleman went through matters of procedure and etiquette and shortly afterwards they were making their way up the Grand Staircase to the magnificent Ballroom.

Small name cards had been placed on the cushioned seats, neatly set out in rows. There was a low murmur of conversation and the atmosphere was charged with a sense of excitement. A small military orchestra from the Household Division was playing Johann Strauss the younger.

At precisely half past eleven, the music stopped, signalling the entrance of the King, accompanied by two Gurkha officers and a procession of Yeomen of the Guard, looking resplendent in their Beefeater uniforms. The Lord Chamberlain began to read out the names of those receiving honours, Georgie gently perspiring as he awaited his turn.

'Mr. George Pillson for services to the arts' called out the Lord Chamberlain, not long afterwards. Georgie sat there, motionless. He had certainly heard his name but, in a slight daze, it had not fully registered.

'Mr. George Pillson,' repeated the Lord Chamberlain and Lucia meaningfully cleared her throat at the back of the room, just loud enough to stir Georgie into action. He rose, approached the King, knelt on the velvet Investiture Stool and was duly knighted and presented with his Insignia. The whole process was over in less than a minute. Georgie returned to his seat, surprisingly exhausted but utterly relieved. The ceremony ended with the National Anthem. It was then announced that the King himself would not be attending the reception afterwards but that the Queen would be hosting the event. It was well known that the King, not in the best of health, had cut back on his list of Royal duties.

Although not particularly warm, the early spring sunshine cast its rays upon the guests as they chatted merrily, numerous waiting staff serving tea and coffee to accompany the abundant selection of finger sandwiches, pastries and cakes.

Lucia, now fully-adjusted to being Lady Pillson, having thought of herself as such ever since Georgie's letter had arrived, was conversing with the wife of a business man awarded an OBE who, she learned, had made his fortune from canning vegetables and provided employment for several hundred workers in the Lincolnshire Wolds. Although Lucia was sure that she had never actually eaten a canned vegetable, she listened politely as the manufacturing process was described in great detail with Lucia adding a 'Really, dear?' and a 'Is that so?' every now and again. It turned out that the lady had worked on the production line during the War, shelling peas and scraping carrots, had caught the eye of the boss and had never handled a vegetable since.

'I started on potatoes, then got promoted to carrots and did such a good job that I moved up to peas,' announced the lady, proudly. Lucia had never considered the hierarchical nature of vegetables before but it seemed rather obvious that the humble potato should be at the bottom. Though perhaps even potatoes had some sort of pecking order – from the earth-clad, eye-ridden chippers found in huge paper sacks to the Jersey Royal, which arrived in Tilling in the late springtime?

Georgie, having begun several awkward and short-lived conversations, was now happily chatting with Foljambe, a cheese straw being waved animatedly as he spoke. Foljambe, true to her position, had earlier attempted, unsuccessfully, to pour their cups of tea. Georgie dearly wished that Olga had been able to accompany them too but she was still in America.

Lucia signalled to Georgie that she was in need of a short break and made her way to the Palace again, looking for the appropriate signage and room. The corridors were deserted as it was 'all hands on deck' outside and Lucia took the opportunity to visit the Picture Gallery and view masterpieces by Rubens, Titian and Van Dyck.

As Lucia made her way to the North Wing of the Palace, again she missed the appropriate sign – this time marked 'Strictly Private' and ventured forth, assuming that she would soon find a bathroom.

As Lucia continued to make her way, she could hear a faint crying coming from one of the rooms at the end of the corridor. As she approached the room the crying got louder. Tentatively, she entered, for the door was open, and saw Princess Elizabeth sat on the edge of the bed, a large handkerchief in her hand.

Looking quite startled, the Princess immediately stood up and moved to the window.

'Your Royal Highness, please forgive me,' croaked Lucia, for the shock was equally felt, 'I was looking for the bathroom.'

The Princess turned and smiled at Lucia.

'It is I who should be apologising for my disposition. There is a bathroom three doors down on the left.'

'Is there anything I can do to help Ma'am. I am Lady Pillson, by the way.'

Princess Elizabeth walked towards Lucia, offered her hand, smiled and signalled for her to sit in the chair opposite. After a brief pause, the Princess spoke.

'It's Father – he is so ill and I do so worry.'

For the next twenty minutes or so, Lucia sat with the young Princess and listened patiently as she spoke. Becoming increasingly candid, Lucia sensed that an *understanding* of some description was developing between them. Perhaps a latent motherly instinct was at play? Lucia had never regretted the fact that she had not had children, yet here she sat, with the heir to the Throne of all people, just as a mother might console her daughter. The Princess managed a smile as Lucia recalled her dear friend Poppy, Duchess of Sheffield who, Lucia was delighted to learn, had been a friend of the Royal Family and used to treat the young Princesses to copious amounts of sweet liquorice and sherbert every Christmas. The conversation ended with the Princess recounting the various exploits of the toddler Prince.

'Thank you, Lady Pillson for listening.'
'It has been an honour, Ma'am. Please do call me Lucia,' and they shook hands once more.
'Three doors down on the left!' called the Princess as Lucia made her way out of the room.

Georgie was conversing with a man in uniform when Lucia returned to the gardens. Although the Colonel's military exploits were nodoubt of considerable merit, Georgie was more interested in his highly-decorated uniform with its intricate needlework and gold braiding.

As she sipped her tea, Lucia reflected that the last half hour – probably the most important thirty minutes in her lifetime, could be shared with no one – not even Georgie. How she would have liked to tell all her Tilling friends that she had spent a good half an hour or so in rapt conversation with the future Queen of England. Imagine their faces when they learnt that the Princess had chosen Lucia to confide in. But no. This was an entirely private matter – and private it would stay.

The clearing up of cups and saucers, together with the

removal of the plates of sandwiches and cakes, signalled the end of the proceedings and the various guests ambled from the garden back to the Palace to collect coats and bags and make their eventual way home.

'It's been a splendid day, Sir,' remarked Foljambe as she climbed into the back seat of the Rolls, sitting next to Lucia this time. Georgie sat in the front, his Insignia proudly on show.

'Well, yes it has,' agreed Georgie, 'Quite splendid!'

'Mrs. Pillson must be so proud of you…. beg your parden, Ma'am…. *Lady* Pillson.'

'No need to fret Foljambe. You'll soon get used to it!' replied Lucia.

A few days later, Lucia received a letter from London with the Royal Crown embossed on the envelope. It was simply signed 'Elizabeth'.

Chapter 8

'Olga's coming back!' exclaimed Georgie. He was sat at his desk, a postcard from New York in his hand.

Having had great success at the Metropolitan Opera, Olga had been asked to revive Cortese's *Lucrezia* at the New York City Opera. She had planned to return to London immediately afterwards but had been lured back to the stage by a wealthy Texan who bankrolled the Fort Worth Opera and was very happy to bankroll Olga too.

'She arrives back in Liverpool on the *Britannic* on Friday and is planning to stay there for the weekend,' continued Georgie.

'Then you must meet her, Georgie! And show her your Insignia.'

'Oh that would be splendid, Lucia!'

'Take the car, Georgie and you might as well ask Foljambe to join you. I'll book three rooms at the Aldelphi Hotel. Cadman and Foljambe deserve a little treat.'

'Are you absolutely sure, Lucia?'

'Of course, Georgie. You will have lots to tell her and I am absolutely certain that she will have lots to tell you. I would join you, if I could, but I have Trust matters to deal with. An empty house will aid my concentration.'

Georgie was in high spirits the following two days at the prospect of seeing Olga again. He couldn't wait to tell her all about the Investiture – after all, it was she who had had the 'quiet word' with the right people and secured his knighthood. He carefully packed his Insignia in his travel case, ready for the visit to Liverpool.

On Thursday afternoon, Georgie, Cadman and Foljambe set off for their destination, a distance of nearly three hundred miles. It was a tedious journey, only occasionally relieved when Cadman was able to put his foot down and unleash the mighty power of the Rolls-Royce engine. As they approached the north-west of the country, the traffic built up considerably and the Liverpool roads were very slow-moving.

They reached the Adelphi Hotel in the late evening and Georgie retired to his room, ordering a plate of ham salad sandwiches through room service. After unpacking their things, Cadman and Foljambe drove to the Woolton Picture House to see *Sunset Boulevard*, finishing their evening off with fish and chips eaten straight from their newspaper wrappings. They both agreed that this was the *only* way to eat the nation's favourite dish.

The next morning, Georgie was up bright and early and breakfasted in the hotel restaurant just before eight. Having eaten lightly the previous day he was now particularly hungry and ordered a full English breakfast, enquiring whether black pudding was included. Georgie adored black pudding though preferred not to think about its origin. By contrast, Lucia hated the stuff and had almost forbade it from entering the kitchen at Mallards. In an unusual compromise, Georgie was allowed black pudding on his birthday, Christmas Eve and on holidays.

After breakfast, Georgie knocked on Cadman and Foljambe's door. There was an uncomfortable moment as Cadman answered, shirtless and Georgie caught a brief glimpse of Foljambe wrapped in a bathing towel.

'Slept in, sir,' mumbled Cadman, 'I'll be ready in five, sir. Shall I meet you in the foyer?'

'Splendid! Thank you,' replied Georgie, adding a rather unnecessary 'Do carry on,' as he strode back to his own room.

As the car made its way to Gladstone Dock, Georgie, looking out of the window, noticed just how vibrant a city Liverpool appeared to be. Bombed heavily in the War, it had undergone somewhat of a transformation as old slums were cleared, replaced by new municipal housing estates and large, impressive Victorian buildings were repaired and renovated. The *Britannic* was already in dock and a steady stream of people could be seen leaving the ship, small bags in hand, larger suitcases being transferred ashore by the crew. Georgie had forgotten just how enormous these trans-Atlantic liners were and there were literally hundreds of passengers milling around, some knowing the correct procedures for disembarkation and exit, but others looking rather dazed and confused.

Georgie need not have worried however, for very soon afterwards he heard his name being trilled out on a top C sharp and spied a hand waving furiously. As he approached, Olga made a dash forward, embraced him, bear-like, kissing him firmly on the cheek.

'Oh Georgie, it's so good to see you again! America's

quite amazing but there is simply nowhere like home!' and she kissed him again.

'I've got so much to tell you,' replied Georgie. 'Let's find Cadman and we'll have a spot of luncheon at the Adelphi. Oh, by the way, Lucia has booked a room for you there.'

'How sweet of dear Lucia. Is she there now?' asked Olga.

'Unfortunately she has had to stay in Tilling. All her charity work, you know.'

Olga's eyes visibly lit up.

'Then, dearest Georgie,' she teased, 'Let's make the most of it!' and she grabbed his arm, dragging him off to find her suitcase.

During a delicious luncheon of crayfish salad at the Adelphi, Olga told Georgie all about her American trip. Despite rave reviews for her performances at the Metropolitan Opera, she had found her fellow cast to be most unfriendly and she had despised her time there. At the New York City Opera, despite a more amiable cast and crew, the schedule had been so demanding that she felt positively exhausted by the end of the run, scuppering her plans of daily sight-seeing.

'Then why didn't you return home?' enquired Georgie.

'Money, Georgie. I can't deny it. Texan money!'

After a short pause, he continued, tentatively.

'And this wealthy Texan?'

'Hideous man, Georgie. Uncultered and louche…but loaded!'

Georgie's eyebrows raised.

'But I could handle him, Georgie and he gave me this as a

parting gift,' and she pulled up the sleeve of her blouse to reveal a dazzling pink diamond bracelet that would not have been out of place in Garrard's front window.

'I must admit, he's got great taste in jewelry, though!' and she gave out one her raucous laughs, just loud enough to catch the attention of the other diners.

That afternoon, as they boated on the lake at Sefton Park, Georgie told Olga all about the Investiture, how nervous he had been beforehand and how he wished that Olga had been able to accompany him to the Palace. As they drifted on the placid waters, Georgie wondered to himself just how different his life might have been if he had married Olga, rather than Lucia. But then, marriage to Olga would have been an entirely different proposition altogether and, on reflection, he was rather content with his current arrangement.

Georgie delved into his pocket and carefully took out his Insignia and passed it to Olga. She looked decidely underwhelmed as she held in between her fingers.

'What a pretty little medal, Georgie, though I would have expected something a bit more imposing for a Knight of the Realm.'

'It's just the right size to fit into my bibelot cabinet,' replied Georgie, slightly irked at Olga's observation.

However, neither had observed the wayward boat that was fast approaching theirs, skippered by two small boys and a sleeping father. Unable to avoid a collision, the boat rammed Georgie and Olga's craft, sending both of them lurching forward and the Isignia went flying into the murky depths of the lake.

'Sorry about that,' said the father, stirred from slumber as the two boys giggled, showing no sense of remorse whatsoever. Georgie stared into the water.

'My Insignia!' was his only response.

Once back on dry land, Olga spoke to the boatman who was slouched by the side of the boathouse, smoking a cigarette. She offered him ten pounds to find 'her pretty necklace', not wishing to alert him to the importance of the missing object.

'It's not worth anything,' she said, 'Just sentimental value. If you find it, bring it to the Adelphi Hotel and you will be able to collect your reward.'

'What am I going to say to Lucia?' asked Georgie, panic beginning to set in.

'Nothing... for the moment,' was her unconvincing reply.

Dinner was a glum affair. Georgie tried to converse politely and show some enthusiasm for Olga's opinions on the social inadequacies of Texan men, but all the time he was thinking about the incident on the boating lake. Perhaps the man had found the Insignia and was on his way, at this very moment, to the hotel? Or perhaps he hadn't even bothered trying to find it, the water being too deep or too cold. How tar'some!

To cheer him up, Olga had promised Georgie a surprise on Saturday. She had spoken to Cadman about the possibility of him taking them both to a football match at

Anfield – Liverpool were playing Wolverhampton Wanderers, but he had suggested that a day at the races might be more to Georgie's liking.

Aintree racecourse was just a few miles from the Adelphi Hotel and in less than twenty minutes, Cadman had transported them there, dropping them off near to the Members' Enclosure, where Olga was greeted enthusiastically.

'Surprised you'll let me back in!' she bellowed to the gate attendant. 'Bagged a seventy-five to one winner last time, Georgie. Went home with nine hundred pounds!'

'Goodness!' exclaimed Georgie as he checked for his wallet.

They were taken to the area specially reserved for owners and trainers and were given two seats almost opposite the finishing post.

'This is just parfect, Olga. What do we do now?'

'Well…' and she pointed out to Georgie the list of races on the racecard, the competing horses and the numerous little booths scattered around the course that housed the bookmakers.

'But I have no idea what horse to pick,' protested Georgie.

Olga gave out one of her hoarse laughs. 'Don't worry at all Georgie. There's no skill involved – it's pure luck!'

Georgie studied the racecard. The first race was at noon. He glanced at the list of the horses and his eye was drawn to one horse in particular *Cavaliero*.

'That's a pretty name. So…Italian!'

'Let's see what the odds are,' said Olga and they made their way to the one of the booths occupied by Herbert Proctor or, as the nameplate stated, 'Honest Herbert'.

'Can give you eight to one on that,' said Mr. Proctor. 'She's got a fair chance, Sir.'

'Is that good?' Georgie asked Olga.

'As good as it gets, Georgie. Get your wallet out!'

Georgie fumbled in his pockets and gave the bookmaker half a crown.

'Last of the big spenders, Georgie!' teased Olga as she passed a ten shilling note to the bookmaker.

'I'll stick it on *Ole Man River,*' and she began to sing the first few lines of the famous song using her lowest possible register.

'Yes, yes!' continued Georgie, 'He just keeps rolling along!' and they returned to their seats, giggling, like a pair of school chums, in the midst of youth.

'Oh well – it was only ten shillings,' remarked Olga as *Monaveen* swept past the winning post and her cheery disposition was maintained throughout the afternoon, despite picking all the wrong horses. Georgie too had failed to back a winner.

'Last race, Georgie. Let's splash out! How about *Benson's Boy* at fifty to one?'

'But we seem to be having a terrible run of bad luck Olga,' Georgie replied, rather concerned.

'Don't believe in luck, Georgie. Never have! Now pass me your wallet – I haven't much left!' and she ran towards Proctor's booth, a wodge of notes in her hand.

'How much, Olga?' asked an exasperated Georgie, as she returned for the start of the race.

She laughed. 'I'll tell you if we win!'

In a matter of minutes, Georgie's wallet could only just cope with his share of the winnings. Olga's luck had turned.

'Almost cleared me out, Sir,' said Mr. Proctor in a resigned voice that indicated that this was not an unusual occurance.

'Oh, I do apologise,' replied a guilt-ridden Georgie.

'All part of the game, Sir. One day you win. One day you loose. Today I lost. Tomorrow, I'll probably win,' and he began to count up the remaining money in his till.

'Dinner's on you tonight then, Georgie,' and Olga grabbed his arm, marching him to where a fleet of taxis were waiting to take the well-to-do winners and losers back home.

Before eating, Georgie and Olga took a stroll around the local streets which, by early evening, were beginning to fill up again.

'Listen Georgie, can you hear that?'

'What?'

'Look, it's coming from over there. That little boy, singing so sweetly, just by the pub on the corner.'

Georgie looked and saw a young boy, probably about ten years old, a hat full of coins by his side, singing *Danny Boy*.

'How sweet!' remarked Olga as she approached him. 'You have a lovely voice, young man. What is your name?'

'John,' replied the boy. 'John Lennon, miss.'

Georgie was amused by his broad Scouse accent.

'Well, John Lennon,' he said, 'This is Miss Olga Bracely and she is a very famous opera singer. If you keep singing, maybe you might become a famous opera star too!' and he gave the boy a shilling.

As they walked to the restaurant, Georgie turned to Olga. 'Destined for the docks, Olga!'

'Oh, Georgie, you're too cruel!' and she gave him a big squeeze. 'You never know – he did have a sparkle in his eye!'

Late that evening, an exhausted Lucia returned to Tilling having spent the previous night in North Norfolk – an unexpected visit that she could hardly have refused. With Cadman in Liverpool, she had had to take a taxi to Hastings, caught the London train and then take a further train to Kings Lynn. Thankfully, a car had been sent to meet her at the station in order to transport her to her final destination. Not wishing to set tongues wagging, Lucia had told Grosvenor that she was going to visit a distant cousin in Eastbourne. Grosvenor had no reason to doubt her.

Chapter 9

As well as divesting her fortune for the benefit of the residents of Tilling, Lucia also intended to use the money to fund some ambitious plans of her own.

At dinner one night, a particularly enjoyable one, as the butcher had been able to supply a haunch of venison which had been roasted in red wine, Lucia brought up the subject of Mallards. She waited whilst Georgie had finished chewing his last forkfull.

'Georgie?'

'Yes, Lucia?' he replied.

'Do you feel settled here?' she continued.

'Why, of course, Lucia. Moving to Tilling from Riseholme was the best thing we ever did.'

'And Mallards?' continued Lucia.

'Such a beautiful house, Lucia. Why Mapp ever agreed to sell it, I'll never know.'

After a little pause, Lucia continued.

'I have been in contact with an architect recently.'

'Yes?'

'And I have asked him to draw up a little plan.'

'Plan, Lucia?'

It was now the time for Lucia to bite the bullet.

'A plan for a new house, Georgie. I think that it's time to move on and leave Mallards.'

For a moment, Georgie was lost for words.

'But Lucia, you love this house!'

'Georgie,' she continued, 'This is not just a whim, it is something that I have considered long and hard, ever since my near-death experience.'

The mention of this stalled Georgie for a moment.

'I have already purchased a small plot of land,' she continued, 'Just past Landgate Street.'

'How small, Lucia?' enquired Georgie, sounding perplexed.

'Six acres, Georgie.'

'Six acres!' exclaimed Georgie. 'Are we to become farmers? Milking cows before breakfast?'

'Grounds, Georgie. Grounds fitting for our new residence…Willows End.'

'Willows End,' repeated Georgie incredulously, 'So this house, which has already been designed, on land that you have already bought, already has a name?'

Lucia could tell that Georgie was angry. Perhaps she should have consulted him right from the start?

'And who is this architect?' asked Georgie, after swilling down the rest of his wine.

'Edward Maufe,' she replied.

Georgie looked blank.

'He designed Guildford Cathedral, Georgie,' added Lucia, in an attempt to win him over.

'Guildford Cathedral! But they've been building that for donkey's years, and it's still not finished!'

'Willows End is not quite on the same scale, Georgie. Mr. Maufe will be using some experimental building techniques that his associates have suggested. The whole building should be ready in three months, once the concrete foundations have been laid,' and she moved to her desk, took out a large roll of paper from the right hand drawer and dramatically unfurled it.

Georgie stared at the architect's drawings. These were no rough sketches but up-to-scale, fully-detailed plans. What had he been expecting? A mock Tudor mansion? A Palladian villa? Instead, Willows End appeared to be a rather large box, enclosing a series of smaller boxes.

'Something fresh, Georgie, something *à la mode*. Mr. Maufe is going to use glass curtain walls downstairs,' and she explained to Georgie that rooms with glass curtain walls didn't need windows. 'It's all the rage in America, apparently.'
Georgie looked horrified.
'But everyone will be able to see inside, Lucia!'
'Nobody will be walking past, Georgie. We shall have uninterrupted views of the countryside, peace and quiet.'

Georgie perused the plans again. Lucia pointed to a small box on the plans for the upper floor which had been intended as an additional study for Lucia.
'Your bibelot room, Georgie.'
'Well a room dedicated to them would be rather nice and presumably I would still have my own sitting-room and bedroom?'
'Of course, Georgie. And perhaps your own library?' she added, as the final sweetener.
Georgie looked at Lucia and the beginnings of a smile stated to appear.

'You still cross with *'ickle* Lucia?'

There was a moment of silence.

'How can I ever be cross with you?'

Once they had eaten dessert, the sale of Mallards was discussed, Lucia having decided that it was better to fully involve Georgie in the process from now on. A figure of six thousand pounds was agreed, a sum that Lucia felt was fair to both vendor and prospective vendee. They would visit Woolgar & Pipstow the following morning.

Neither Mr. Woolgar or Mr. Pipstow were in the office when the Pillsons arrived there shortly before ten o' clock. Instead, a spotty youth who introduced himself as Mr. Sparrow had been left in charge.

'I have full authority to deal with all matters, sir,' said Mr. Sparrow. It's Mr. and Mrs….?'

'Sir George and Lady Pillson, actually, young man,' cut in Georgie. 'From Mallards House.'

'Of course, Sir. How can we help you?'

After a brief discussion, it was agreed that Mallards should be put up for sale at five thousand, nine hundred and ninety-nine pounds with a separate agreement for carpets and soft furnishings. Mr. Sparrow made arrangements to call round in the afternoon and take all the necessary measurements and some photographs. A *For Sale* sign would be placed outside the following day and the property would feature in the next *Hampshire Argus*. Mr. Sparrow also intended to advertise Mallards in some of the London quality press – given that the property was of particularly fine quality.

Returning home, Lucia called for both Grosvenor and Foljambe. Georgie stood by Lucia's side as she addressed them both. He found it difficult to look Foljambe straight in the eye, staring at the patterns in the carpet instead. Lucia did not soften the blow.

'Tomorrow you will see a *For Sale* sign appear outside Mallards.'

Both ladies looked taken aback.

'A new house is going to be built for Sir George and myself.'

Seeing their distress, Georgie spoke in his most soothing voice.

'We are staying in Tilling and very much hope that you will join us when we move.'

'Grosvenor, you will have your own room in the new house and Foljambe, you and Cadman will have your very own flat above the garage and workshop. I hope that is satisfactory,' Lucia continued.

'Oh yes, Miss!' replied Foljambe, the prospect of brand new living quarters sounding very appealing.

Grosvenor's response, however, was rather more muted. Moving house was always fairly traumatic in her experience, for both the owner and the servants. She had become very attatched to Mallards and had hoped to end her working days there. Now there would be all the upheaval, disruption and uncertainty of moving.

'If that's all, Ma'am, I have some jobs to finish,' and Grosvenor left the room.

The erection of the *For Sale* sign coincided with the peak time for daily marketing, so within half an hour of the notice appearing, anyone who had the remotest interest in the affairs of Sir George and Lady Pillson, knew that they planned to leave Mallards.

Collectively making their way to Diva's tea-shop, the Mapp-Flints, the Wyses, Evie and Reverend Bartlett together with Quaint Irene were each expostulating their own theories as to why and where Lucia and Georgie were moving to. Welcoming them all with open arms, the question 'Any news?' brought a riotous response. Diva served up tea and a brand new savoury dish that she had seen recently in *Woman's Weekly*.

'What is that, Diva?' enquired Mapp, as a large serving plate was placed on the table.

'Quiche, Elizabeth. Broccoli and onion. They eat it in all the top London restaurants, according to Janet,' answered Diva.

'The fount of all knowledge!' Mapp mouthed to Susan.

'It looks absolutely delicious, dear. Do cut me a small slice – just to test it.'

Diva listened out especially for the last four words. It was Mapp's way of saying that she didn't intend to pay for it. But today, that did not bother Diva. There was going to be a good hour of gossip to be had, at least.

It wasn't long before news of Willows End became common knowledge in Tilling and the whole of East

Sussex. As a team of workers literally set up camp in the fields by Landgate Street, a veritable collection of diggers, trucks, cranes, cement mixers and various pieces of other building equipment, began to appear alongside.

The architect, Mr. Maufe, had set a very tight schedule for the build and within two weeks of the first sod being cut, a reinforced-concrete base had been constructed on which the whole building would rest. A spell of good weather helped speed up the process enormously.

Two American engineers had been contracted to oversee certain aspects of the build and were staying in relative luxury at the Royal Victoria Hotel in St. Leonards-on-Sea, for the duration of the construction period, having entirely dismissed any notion of residing at the Trader's Arms. Mr. Maufe himself made weekly visits to Tilling, calling at Mallards for his consultations with Lucia. She, in turn, was in regular telephone contact with the architect's office, suggesting various alterations and making additional requests.

Most of these had been entirely reasonable, relating to internal finishing, floor coverings, additional lighting and so on. However, requests to enlargen rooms or even create brand new ones were simply not possible, as Mr. Maufe patiently explained to his client. At times Lucia wished that she had consulted more with Georgie and not rushed ahead impulsively on her own. But, then again, Georgie's natural procrastination might have scuppered the whole idea entirely.

As the building work progressed, Diva, Quaint Irene, the Wyses, Bartletts and Mapp-Flints made regular visits to the site. There was always something new to see and once the glass curtain walling had arrived direct from the Pilkington factory, onlookers were amazed by the rapid progress of the construction. Indeed, pictures of the build appeared in both the *Hampshire Argus* and *The Architectural Review* which asserted that the house was one of the most exciting private residences to be built in the whole of England. Both Lucia and Georgie visited Willows End almost every day and Georgie occasionally took little treats for the workers – bags of aniseed balls, sherbert lemons and Pontefract cakes, not unlike the King, Georgie thought, distributing Maunday money to his subjects.

'It won't be too long before we are gazing outside from *inside* the building, Lucia, rather than gazing inside from the outside,' Georgie quipped.

'Indeed, Georgie. I believe that the roof is due to be commissioned next week and once the building is watertight, the electricians, plumbers and plasterers can begin work.'

'Should I begin to pack my bibelots, Lucia?'
'Soon, Georgie. Soon!'

Chapter 10

The clang of the iron letterbox signalled that the morning post had arrived. Beating Grosvenor to the front door, Lucia scooped up the pile of envelopes that were scattered on the floor – at least a dozen or so.

'Were you expecting so much post?' enquired Grosvenor.

'Most certainly,' replied Lucia, 'My Charitable Trust is now in full operation and I expect there will be many requests for funding.'

Lucia carried the bundle of letters to her desk, on which she had placed a set of document trays marked 'Requests', 'Granted', 'Refused' and 'Pending'.

Before opening any of the envelopes, she scrutinized the handwriting on the front of each and made two piles.

The first pile contained requests from various persons unknown to Lucia. Addresses confirmed that they were residents of Tilling and thus eligible for funds, if granted. A Mr. Simmons asked for fifteen pounds to repair the roof of the pigeon shed on the municipal housing estate on the outskirts of Tilling. Granted. Lucia had no interest in pigeons whatsoever, but knew that these winged creatures brought a great deal of pleasure to the working man. Lucia placed the letter in the appropriate tray. Mrs. Spooner requested five pounds to settle a veterinary bill for her elderly cat, Grubbles. She had lost her husband at the end of the War and had struggled financially ever since. Granted. Lucia made a mental note to send the lady an additional five pounds. Similar pleas for funds amounted to the grand total of thirty-eight pounds, seven shillings and sixpence. Hardly breaking the bank mused Lucia. Now to the more interesting pile!

A pale blue envelope, with a perfectly placed stamp contained the following:

My dearest Lady Pillson,

First of all, Susan and myself would again like to congratulate Sir George on his Royal recognition for services to the arts. As a Member of the Most Excellent Order of the British Empire herself, Susan would be only happy to advise Sir George on any matters of State.

Secondly, we humbly offer whatever help we can muster in relation to your impending move to the new house, the construction of which we have taken a personal interest in. Susan is most proficient in wrapping fine china.

Thirdly, we both commend your good self for the establishment of 'The Lady Pillson Charitable Trust', which this letter concerns.

As you are aware, congestion on the roads is an issue of national importance and our dear Tilling is not immune to the problem. Only the other day, the Royce, which Susan relies on for her transportation into Tilling, was scraped by a passing car for there is nowhere for it to be parked apart from the street itself. This must be seen as the tip of the iceburg.

I would like to draw your attention to a small plot of land that is currently being advertised as being for sale behind the Bank. It would, with appropriate surface works, make an excellent car park for the benefit of all Tilling residents and their vehicles. I believe that offers over one thousand pounds are being invited.

Your, with lasting affection,

Algernon Wyse.

Whilst it was certainly correct that the numbers of vehicles on the local roads was gradually increasing, carnage on the high street was not yet a major issue. And the fact remained that Mrs. Wyse's journey from Starling Cottage in Porpoise Street to the High Street shops was such a brief one that it was quicker to walk then travel by car.

Lucia opened a cream envelope next. Omitting any semblance of formality it read:

Dear Lucia,

As you are offering I thought I would ask. Wasters too small for viable tea-shop. Extention required. Will benefit all.

P.S. Industrial oven required too.

Yours,

Diva.

P.P.S. A local builder is pricing up the job tomorrow.

'What cheek!' thought Lucia as she pictured the horrifying prospect of an industrial oven churning out industrial-sized sardine tartlets.

A vivid yellow envelope contained a request from Quaint Irene for funds to purchase a redundant agricultural building which would be turned into an artistic 'space' housing a collection of original Coles. An interesting prospect thought Lucia. But surely, Miss Coles now had the necessary means to afford this herself? The final letter, contained within a mauve envelope, included a veritable list of 'wanted' items from the Padre and Evie – most of a dubious ecclesiastical nature.

Georgie entered the room. He had been in his sitting-room all morning, polishing his bibelots – a task that he now always undertook personally, following an unfortunate incident involving Foljambe and an over-adventurous feather duster.

'How is the Charity work going, Lucia?' Georgie asked, eyeing the pile of letters placed in the 'Granted' tray.

'Splendidly, Georgino mio!' chirped Lucia. 'It is so rewarding to be able to help those who, for whatever circumstances, are unable to help themselves.'

'Talking of helping themselves, anything from Mapp and the Major?'

'Nothing so far, Georgie but Mr. Wyse, dear Diva, Quaint Irene and the Padre have….' She paused dramatically, '…requested funds,' and she passed Georgie the letters.

As Georgie read each one in turn, his disposition became increasingly agitated, his face reddening. At last, he could contain his anger no longer.

'An industrial oven? A new sofa for the Rectory? Two thousand pounds for an old ramshackle barn? This is preposterous Lucia! And as for the car park, well, most residents of Tilling don't even possess a car!'

'Dear Georgie, you mustn't berate our dear friends, but I suppose you do have a point.'

'So you'll turn down their requests?'

Lucia turned to look at Georgie, gimlet eyes sparkling, 'Pending, Georgie. Pending.'

At Grebe, the Major was on his hands and knees, his upper half ensconced in the cupboard below the kitchen sink. His better half had noticed that the drain was again blocked, most likely caused by Withers' habit of peeling potatoes under a running tap. Mapp had considered calling the plumber but that was an unwelcome expense and she was sure that Benjy, with all his army training, could handle a u-bend and spanner.

'Is it nearly done?' asked Mapp expectantly, crossing her fingers for a positive answer.

'Just got to tighten up this joint, old girl, and everything will be tickety-boo.'

'Marvellous!' exclaimed Mapp adding that the Major would be fully deserving of a chota peg.

'Quai hai!' bellowed the Major as he placed the spanner in the drawer reserved for oddments, 'A chota peg Withers – and make it a large one.'

'Just a pot of tea for me, Withers, thank you,' added Mapp.

As they set down to their respective beverages, Elizabeth glanced around the room. How dreary Grebe seemed. The wallpaper was beginning to peel away in one top corner of the room, slight traces of damp could be spotted underneath the window sills and sections of carpet were worn and dangerously close to becoming threadbare. Of course, an eagle-eye was needed to spot these minor defects, but Mapp possessed one and it was drawn to Grebe's failing fabric.

Quite the opposite of her former home, Mallards, which she had sold to Lucia for a ridiculously low figure. Hailed as one of the finest houses in East Sussex and now being sold once again, every single time she walked past it, she felt a longing to return there. If she could buy it back from Lucia she would have made every attempt but the price Lucia was asking was far in excess of what she and Benjy could afford.

'Everything alright, Liz-girl?' enquired the Major, noticing her sad disposition and absent stare.
'Just thinking, Benjy.'
He waited for an elaboration but none was forthcoming.
'About…?'
'Oh, just life in general,' and she made to dab her eye with the napkin.
'Now, now, Elizabeth. What on earth is the matter?' asked the Major, becoming somewhat concerned as tears began to flow down Mapp's cheeks.
'Why is life so unfair, Benjy? Lucia has everything – a title, a new mansion and even her own Charity. What have we got? A ruin of a house and a pitiful income!' and she began to sob, uncontrollably.
'There, there, Liz-girl. Happiness is not having what you

want but wanting what you have. Grebe isn't so bad and you've always got me.'

If the last comment was meant to comfort Mapp it did not quite do the trick and her sobs became even louder. The Major decided it was best to leave Elizabeth alone for a while and instructed Withers to take in a fresh pot of tea.

Chapter 11

Lucia and Georgie sat in the back of the Rolls-Royce, Cadman taking them once again to the Capital. That afternoon they were to unveil the 'Pillson Aureus' at the British Museum and were meeting Olga beforehand at the Savoy Hotel on the Strand. On entering the hotel, they were told that Miss Bracely was waiting for them in the American Bar, where she had already conveniently ordered a bottle of Champagne.

As Lucia and Georgie entered the Bar, Olga jumped down off her stool, ran towards them arms outstretched and managed successfully to hug them both simultaneously.

'Darlings!' she exclaimed and promptly curtseyed to Lucia. 'May I call you Lucia, Lady Pillson?' she teased.

'Why Olga, *nulla è cambiato!* I remain simple Lucia to all my dearest friends.'

'Glad to have that settled,' replied Olga, 'I'm not one for titles, myself,' and she returned to her bar stool. 'Come and have some Champagne,' she called, catching the attention of the rather handsome young barman.

'Tell me all about this aureus, Georgie,' asked Olga. 'What a discovery! Who actually found it?'

Lucia had already mentioned to friends that Georgie had discovered the coin but not wishing to utter an untruth, especially to Olga, he merely replied that Lucia had discovered the coin – which she had, in a way, but not at the bottom of the garden!

Lucia could not resist elaborating.

'Yes, I remember that the excavations had been yielding little for several days and I had considered abandoning them. I had been digging for hours and was about to stop entirely when my trowel hit something hard.'

'How exciting!' replied Olga, 'And...?'

'A dear little box – probably bronze, which contained the aureus. Of course, at the time I had no idea of its importance and I simply put it away. I must confess that I had forgotten all about it until dear Elizabeth Mapp-Flint introduced me to Mr. Chesworth, that delightful young man from the British Museum. Dear Elizabeth, always such a help.'

Georgie could not quite believe what he was hearing and decided to remain entirely silent.

After one more glass of Champagne, the trio made their way to Cadman and the waiting Rolls-Royce, ready for their ten minute journey to the Britsih Museum. Out of sight of Lucia, Olga passed Georgie a little paper bag.

'You might be needing this today, Georgie,' whispered Olga. Georgie's eyes lit up as he took a peak inside the bag. There was his Insignia.

'They only found it a few days ago. The boat man took it straight to the Adelphi. The Hotel Manager posted it on to me. I've given it a good clean!'

'Oh, Olga! Thank you!' and he kissed her gently on the cheek. 'I'll pin it on when we get to the Museum.'

In the Department of Coins and Medals, the Curator, Mr.

Sampson Guy, a dapper gentleman of middle age who sported a perfectly groomed handlebar moustache, was already waiting for them, accompanied by Mr. Chesworth who had originally authenticated the coin. Mr. Chesworth shook hands enthusiastically with the trio. He had already published a paper on the coin which had appeared in *The Historian* and had been invited to give several lectures on the discovery. A small crowd of dignitaries were gathered alongside a press photographer and a reporter from *The Telegraph*. Lucia had expected a rather larger crowd, after all Georgie was now a Trustee of the Museum and the aureus was of national importance.

With a clearing of the throat and a look at his wristwatch, the Curator signalled the start of the ceremony, which Lucia had now realised was going to be a rather low-key affair.

'Distinguished guests, I am delighted to welcome Sir George and Lady Pillson to the British Museum for the unveiling of the 'Pillson Aureus', most generously donated to the Nation. Found at the home of Sir George and Lady Pillson, this rare coin reminds us of our ancient past as we recall Roman Britain in all its glory. Please, Sir George, will you do the honours?' and invited Georgie to step forward.

A little pair of red velvet curtains parted as Georgie expertly pulled an a-joining chord, revealing the gold aureus placed in the centre of the plaque, the design of which was tastefully simple. Underneath there was a small inscription which read:

For the benefit of the Nation, the Pillson Aureus, most generously donated by

Lady Emmeline Pillson

and Sir George Pillson, Bart.

There was a gentle round of applause as Georgie looked at the inscription again. He turned to catch Lucia's eye, but she was already engaged in a vivid conversation with the reporter.

Olga noticed Georgie's expression of annoyance.
'What's up, Georgie?' she asked, matter-of-fact, as always.
'Well,' he mumbled, 'I appear to have been rather belittled in the inscription.'
'No!' exclaimed Olga. 'There must be some mistake. I'll have a word with Mr. Guy.'
Georgie shook his head. 'I rather think that Lucia has already had a word,' as he remembered a half-heard telephone conversation between his wife and Mr. Guy the previous month. When she had said 'Sir George won't mind a bit,' he hadn't realised that Lucia was, in fact, discussing something that Sir George *would* mind a great deal. It seemed that Lucia had been prepared to be publicly acknowledged as Emmeline (a name she detested) for the sake of immortality.
'Well it's a bad show, Georgie,' Olga continued. 'Sometimes I think that Lucia doesn't deserve you.'
Georgie blushed. Perhaps Olga was right – she often was.

'Over here, Georgie!' called Lucia, who was standing with Mr. Guy alongside the 'Pillson Aureus'. The press photographer was ready and waiting with his camera. He needed to make a sharp exit in order to make his next rendezvous in the West End, where the Cambridge Theatre was re-opening, having just been extensively refurbished.

'I'll stand on this side with Mr. Guy and you can stand on the other side.'

'Shall I ask Olga to join us?' enquired Georgie.

Lucia gave Georgie a look.

'I don't think that that is necessary, Georgie,' and she smiled gracefully at the camera, as Olga looked on from a distance.

Afterwards, Mr. Guy ushered everyone into a side room where a modest buffet had been laid, presumably some time earlier, as some of the sandwiches were beginning to curl up at the edges.

A stern-faced lady stood by an urn of boiling water. She filled a large teapot, gave it a quick stir and began pouring the tea into the line of cups adjacent to the urn.

'Georgie, this sandwich looks so old, I think it could actually be an exhibit!' remarked Olga, mouth half-full.

'Try a sausage roll – they're rather tasty,' said Mr. Guy, who had sidled up to them both and had managed to cram as much food as possible onto his small plate, the stated article balanced precariously on top of a pile of sandwiches. 'We get them direct from the kitchens at Pentonville Prison.'

'You mean that the criminals make the sausage rolls?'

asked a startled Georgie.

'Of course, Sir George! They do a roaring trade in London. All the top hotels and restaurants serve Pentonville 'specials'. And don't forget that if it weren't for legions of criminals, many of the exhibits on show here today might still be in their rightful place of origin,' and he gave Olga a wink. Georgie wasn't sure whether Mr. Guy was being serious or speaking tongue in cheek.

'Well, they are rather delicious, Mr. Guy,' said Olga, little flakes of pastry stuck to her lips.

Olga had had to leave mid-afternoon as she was meeting Sir Thomas Beecham in Mayfair to discuss an upcoming engagement with the Royal Philharmonic Orchestra.

'Tea at The Ritz, Georgie? We have a couple of spare hours before Cadman is due back,' suggested Lucia.

'I'm really not that hungry, Lucia. I rather over-indulged earlier. Too many sausage rolls!'

'Then how about a walk by the Thames?'

'Splendid idea, Lucia!'

'We could take a boat trip?'

'I'd rather not, today,' replied Georgie, visions of his Insignia sinking to the depths of the boating lake in Sefton Park returning briefly.

As they walked by the riverside, Georgie contemplated rebuking Lucia over the inscription. He was used to playing second fiddle in their relationship but, on consideration, it was better to play second fiddle than have no fiddle at all. As if she was reading his thoughts, Lucia spoke.

'Did you notice anything odd about the inscription, Georgie?' asked Lucia.

'Well I didn't really take much notice of it, Lucia,' replied Georgie, lying through his teeth. 'What was the matter?'

'Just a small sizing issue with the text, Georgie. I'll have a word with Mr. Guy and see if we can get it changed.'

Georgie swallowed hard.

'No need to make a fuss, Lucia. Now let's get on with our walk! We don't want Cadman thinking we have got lost!'

Chapter 12

Arriving back at Mallards just before midnight, Lucia had left a note for Grosvenor not to disturb both Georgie and herself until ten in the morning. Therefore Grosvenor served a late breakfast the following day which Lucia and Georgie duly ate just before eleven.

It was another hot, sunny day and neither Lucia or Georgie had any particular plans. Lucia called for Grosvenor.

'Can you set out two chairs in the *giardino segreto* please Grosvenor. Georgie and I shall be engaged in some quiet activities for the next few hours. And,' she added, 'Would you prepare some fruit cordial.'

'Right you are Ma'am,' replied Grosvenor. 'And after that would you mind if I went out for an hour, Ma'am? Mrs. Plaistow's Janet wants to look over some new recipes for the tea-shop.

'Probably some gigantic pie to pop into her industrial oven,' quipped Georgie.

As Lucia and Georgie sat in the midday sun, Lucia flicking through Dante and Georgie applying a delicate Florentine stitch to his own needlepoint design of wild horses at sunset, Mapp was making her way to Mallards, envelope in hand. Enclosed was a request for money to pay for the laying of new drains leading up to Grebe. The Town Council had already surveyed the area and a Mr. Ratchett from the Works Department had told the Major that although new drainage was desirable, as Grebe was right at the end of the proposed pipework, the job was 'on hold' for the forseable future. Mapp didn't expect her request to be successful, but, as the Major had said, there was always a chance!

She knocked on the front door and waited for Grosvenor to answer. As Grosvenor had left Mallards five minutes previously, a second knock brought no response. Expecting the door to be locked, she tried it anyway. To her surprise it had been left open and she entered cautiously.

Seeing that nobody was about – Foljambe was spending a day at Hastings with Cadman, she made her way into the hall, poking her head through the doors of several different rooms. As she entered the garden-room she could hear raised voices outside. She followed the path to the *giardino segretto* and was just about to enter it, through the arch, when she heard something that made her ears positively prick up. She stood, unseen, behind the laurel bush, listening intently.

Lucia and Georgie were not having an argument as such but a disagreement of a substantial nature. Georgie had earlier broken a needle and then had spilt blackcurrant cordial on his tapestry. Both these incidents had darkened his mood. He had then reacted angrily to Lucia's suggestion that she might publish a book about Mallards' Roman hoard, accusing her of not just embroidering the truth but telling a complete pack of lies.

'If the truth were known, I cannot imagine the consequences Lucia. I could be stripped of my knighthood!'

Lucia, for once, looked rather sheepish.

'All for one-upmanship! Why you ever wasted all that money on that silly coin, I'll never know. And from a dodgy dealer too!'

Lucia was about to refute the last comment but then remembered that the coin was sold without provenance and she had destroyed all documentation relating to the purchase.

Georgie huffed. 'Oh, I don't wish to mention it ever again. The whole business has left a nasty taste in my mouth.'

'Try a little blackcurrant cordial, Georgie,' replied Lucia, in a failed attempt to lighten the atmosphere. Georgie was not amused.

As the two continued to exchange views, Mapp's mouth gradually opened wider and wider, almost to the point of pain. However, a beaming smile appeared soon afterwards. 'I've got her this time,' thought Mapp, 'Good and proper!' She tip-toed back to the house, a master-plan beginning to formulate in her mind. Such was her elation, she failed to see Grosvenor on the opposite side of the street, returning to Mallards.

After changing back into her uniform, Grosvenor made her way to the garden.

'Any more drinks needed, Ma'am?' she asked.

'No thank you, Grosvenor. We have adequate supplies for the moment.'

'If I had known you were expecting company, I would have put Janet off until this afternoon, with your permission, of course, Ma'am.'

Lucia gave Georgie a quizzical look.

'Visitors, Grosvenor?'

'Mrs. Mapp-Flint, Ma'am. She was coming out of the front door just as I came back.'

Georgie gave Lucia a look verging on horror. Grosvenor must have left the door open by mistake. However, now was not the time to chastise Grosvenor as Lucia did not want to give her the impression that anything was wrong.

'Oh yes, Grosvenor. Dear Elizabeth just popped round on Charity business. Now, as Foljambe is away today, would you mind attending to Sir George's sitting room?'

Once Grosvenor had returned to the house it was safe to talk.

'Lucia, you know what this means, don't you?' Georgie was visibly upset.

Lucia sat, fingers perched on the bridge of her nose – a pose which always indicated a situation of the upmost gravity.

'I need a few minutes to think, Georgie.'

At Grebe, Mapp poured herself a sweet sherry – a treat in usual circumstances, but a necessity at this present time. She had been right all along. There were never any Roman ruins at Mallards, the whole thing a concoction conjured up by Lucia for the sake of self-glorification.

And how could Georgie – a Knight of the Realm – go along with it all? Anything could be expected of Lucia, but not Georgie!

As she pondered the failings of men in general, Benjy entered the room. He had been under the kitchen sink again, his previous tightening of the joint not quite as tight as it should have been.

'Did you give her the letter, Liz-girl?' he enquired.

'It never quite got to that stage, Benjy-boy,' she replied.

The Major looked puzzled.

"I'll tell you everything at dinner, I promise,' and she called for Withers, instructing her to visit the poulterer, roast a large chicken, prepare a delicious fruit pudding, serve it with lots of double cream and open one of the few remaining bottles of Wrotham Pinot, reserved for very special occasions.

'Of course, ma'am. Very good ma'am,' replied Withers in an unusually cheerful voice, the prospect of a tasty feast lightening her mood.

Having moved into the house, Lucia and Georgie were still discussing their uninvited guest.

'She might just have entered the house and gone straight back out when she realised that nobody was about,' said Georgie, unconvincingly. 'We don't actually know that she heard anything.'

'I fear the worst, Georgie,' confessed Lucia, 'We are going to have to pay for this.'

'You don't think that she will resort to asking for money, do you? That's tantamount to blackmail! No! It *is* blackmail!'

'Georgie, what choice do we have if she does? If we refuse her demands then she will let everyone know that the aureus wasn't found amongst the Roman ruins at Mallards!'

Georgie was exasperated.

'Lucia! There *were* no Roman ruins and ......' He hesitated. He wanted to tell her that she was indeed a fraud, but simply didn't have the heart to utter the truth.

'We need a plan, Georgie.'

'It needs to be a damned good one, Lucia!' replied Georgie.

That evening, whilst the Mapp-Flints enjoyed a splendid dinner, Benjy now fully informed of the day's events and discoveries, Sir George and Lady Pillson sat at the dinner table in silence, the food almost untouched.

Chapter 13

How long would she have to wait? Lucia sat in the garden-room, gazing out onto the High Street for the inevitable approach of Mapp. Elizabeth, if she were true to form, would be knocking on Mallards' door, making her demands, that very morning. But what if she didn't do the obvious thing? She could keep Lucia dangling for however long she desired, a spider sat contentedly at the edge of its web, ready to pounce!

'I'll let her stew,' thought Mapp as she finished her morning cup of tea, telling Benjy that she would leave her visit to Lucia till the late afternoon. But sheer excitement and anticipation got the better of her and she left for Mallards soon after luncheon.

By the time Mapp knocked on the door of Mallards House, Lucia had long abandoned her look-out post and was attempting *The Times* crossword in an unsuccessful bid to distract herself from the impending battle. Three across: act of surrender. Lucia reluctantly scrawled *capitulation*.

Grosvenor answered the door.
'Why, Mrs. Mapp-Flint, Lady Pillson did say that she might be expecting you. Do come in.'
Mapp strode purposefully through the hallway and into the garden-room.

'Lucia, darling! Grosvenor tells me that you were expecting my company.'

'Why Elizabeth, dear, I did have an inkling that you might pay me a visit. I had morning tea ready for you, earlier.'

'Never mind dear, I just had a delightful lunch with my dear Benjy-boy. I didn't want to rush things.'

Lucia looked Mapp straight in the eye.

'Rush things, dear?'

Oblivious to the last question, Mapp began to rummage in her capacious handbag and eventually retrieved a fresh newspaper clipping.

'I saw this lovely photograph today in *The Telegraph*,' and passed the paper to Lucia.

It was a report on the unveiling of the 'Pillson Aureus', describing in great detail how the coin had been found, accompanied by a photograph of Lucia, Georgie and Mr. Sampson Guy, Curator of The Department of Coins and Medals at the British Museum.

'Wasn't sure whether you had seen it yet, dear,' said Mapp. 'I expect that it will appear in the *Hampshire Argus* later in the week.'

'How thoughtful of you, Elizabeth,' replied Lucia.

'It's so gratifying to know that my dear Mallards now has a place in history…inperpetuity,' trilled Mapp, the last word given a particular emphasis.

'Maybe a cup of tea would be nice, after all and some of those delicious chocolate buscuits you have. Just plain old custard creams left at the Mapp-Flint household, I'm afraid!

After Grosvenor had been called, Lucia sat nervously as she awaited Mapp's next move. After a short pause, Mapp continued.

'Old friends as we are, Lucia, I feel that we can share a little secret.'

'Secret, dear?'

'Well, quite a *molto segreto* actually! But, never mind, I am certain that we can come to some… arrangement.'

'Arrangement, dear?'

'As Mallards is up for sale, it would be my dearest wish to come back here. Dear Aunt Caroline would turn in her grave if I didn't seize the opportunity to return.'

'Is that so, Elizabeth?' responded Lucia.

'But your asking price is just a few pennies more than we can stretch to.'

'And...?' enquired Lucia.

'If you were to purchase Grebe for, say, seven thousand pounds, I could then afford to buy Mallards.'

Lucia swallowed hard.

'But Mallards is on the market for *six* thousand pounds and your valuation of Grebe seems…' She paused.

'…Highly inflated, Elizabeth.' She had wanted to say that Mapp's valuation of Grebe was utterly ridiculous but could not afford to rouse Elizabeth's ire.

'Lulu, what is a few pounds amongst friends?' adding, ominously 'Friends with secrets!'

Lucia swallowed again. A hideous analogy, but she felt rather like a cow awaiting to be poleaxed.

'And friends with secrets never tell?' Lucia enquired gently.

After a moment's thought, Lucia heard the words that she was so desperate to hear.

'Never!' replied Mapp, resolutely. 'My lips are sealed,' and she grinned inanely.

At this response, Lucia's mood lifted a little.

'Then everything appears to be in order, Elizabeth, dear.' She moved to her desk, opened the left-hand drawer and extracted a book of cheques. She bit her lip as she signed the cheque *Lady Emmeline Pillson* but, otherwise, finished the transaction with due grace.

'I shall contact my solicitor tomorrow morning,' said Mapp, 'And get the ball rolling. Of course, I wouldn't want you to have to move out straight away.'

'That's very thoughtful of you, dear,' replied Lucia, 'The builders have not yet finished Willows End.'

''I'll give you a month!' was Mapp's curt reply as Grosvenor entered, carrying a tray of tea and buscuits. Ignoring the requested refreshments, she strode out of the garden-room, clutching the cheque, and made her way straight to the bank.

All this time, Georgie had been in his sitting-room, not wishing to be part of the proceedings. It was Lucia who had brought about this mess and it was she who should jolly well sort it out. On hearing the front door being shut, he tentatively came downstairs.

'Has she gone?' he asked.

'Yes, Georgie.'

'Did she know about the aureus?'

'She didn't mention it directly, Georgie, but it was quite obvious that she had heard our conversation yesterday.'

'Did she ask for money?'

'Not exactly.'

'Then what on earth did she want?'

Lucia looked at Georgie and then looked around the room, her arms indicating its four corners. At first, Georgie did not seem to comprehend but then it hit him, right between the eyes.

'No!' he gasped and threw himself down onto the sofa. He began to shake his head and Lucia wondered if she ought to go and comfort him.

'She's got exactly what she has always wanted, Lucia. And you could do nothing to stop her. Actually, my hat goes off to her!'

'Georgie!' cried Lucia.

'Oh let's be realistic, Lucia. Her actions are no worse than yours – and she's no Lady! Let us hope that she keeps her word and doesn't spill the beans.'

'Georgie, I've already thought of that and I think I have a plan!'

'Well it needs to be a good one – my knighthood's at stake, not to mention our good reputation!'

'Tourists, Georgie,' was the reply.

Tilling, with its cobbled streets and pretty houses, had become quite a draw in the summer months, with its close proximity to Hastings.

'Tourists? Tar'some folk. Always asking directions to the nearest public convenience.'

'An exhibition,' continued Lucia.

'An exhibition?'

'Of the Roman ruins and the discovery of the aureus.'

Georgie tutted loudly.

'There are no ruins, Lucia and you never discovered any aureus!' he reminded her once again. Lucia carried on regardless.

'If Mapp were to open up the gardens of Mallards in the summer months for the tourists to see the exact spot where the aureus was discovered, not only would she gain a very useful income, but it would guarantee that she keeps quiet. It would be in her own interest to maintain that the aureus was found in Tilling.'

Georgie pondered this proposition for a moment.

'I see. But how do we get her to do it?'

'I will simply tell the Wyses, the Bartletts, Diva and Quaint Irene that I had considered the possibility of opening up Mallards to the public but had abandoned the idea due to possible excessive crowds. I will insist that they don't mention this to Elizabeth – we don't want to give her ideas, do we?'

'Parfect, Lucia! Mapp's bound to take the bait!'

The following day, Lucia visited Woolgar & Pipstow to sign essential papers. Mr. Pipstow had telephoned Mallards earlier that morning to say that an offer had been received.

'What a turn up for the books, Lady Pillson,' said Mr. Pipstow, 'Mrs. Mapp-Flint returning to Mallards House. If you don't mind me saying, Lady Pillson, you could stall the process a little and wait for a higher offer. We have had some interest from the provinces. Mr. Sparrow has had one or two expressions of interest.'

'Dear Mr. Pipstow, I have already given my word to Mrs. Mapp-Flint. Please proceed with the sale.'

'Of course, Lady Pillson. Mallards House sold for five thousand, eight hundred and fifty pounds.'

Had she heard correctly?

'Not the asking price, Mr. Pipstow?'

'No. Mrs. Mapp-Flint felt that to be a fair offer.'

Lucia stopped herself from responding.

'And Mrs. Mapp-Flint requested that these items be included in the sale. Mostly large pieces of furniture that she had to leave behind when she moved out to Grebe,' and he handed Lucia a list, neatly typed and efficiently addressed 'To the Vendor'.

'I do believe I purchased these items as part of the original sale,' said Lucia as she quickly scanned the list, 'Dear Elizabeth, so absent-minded at times. I'll have a word with her Mr. Pipstow,' and she made to leave the office.

As she made her way along the High Street she spied Diva advancing towards her at great pace. For one moment, Lucia thought about escaping into the nearest shop but decided to stand her ground instead.

'Lucia! Lucia!' cried Diva, her pace increasing to a veritable trot. 'Is is true? Mapp's bought Mallards?'

'How quickly news travels Diva, dear. When did Elizabeth tell you?'

'So it *is* true. Haven't seen Mapp yet. Quaint Irene told me last night. She bumped into Mr. Wyse who had been told by the Padre.'

'My thunder has been stolen,' replied Lucia. 'So happy to be passing Mallards back to my dear friend, Elizabeth.'

'But is your new house ready Lucia?'

'Not quite finished yet, Diva. Grebe will be our abode for a few months once the sale has completed.'

'Grebe?' enquired Diva.

'Yes, Diva. In order to facilitate the sale, I offered to purchase Grebe from Elizabeth.'

'She must have bitten your hand off, Lucia!'

'Elizabeth's bark is far worse than her bite, Diva, dear! Au reservoir!'

As she walked back to Mallards, Lucia's demeanour seemed calm enough, though inside she was positively seething.

Chapter 14

It was the day of the move. Elizabeth was excited. She had risen at five and had spent a few more precious hours finishing the jobs that she had abandoned the previous evening as the midnight chimes rang. Benjy had been very helpful initially, but after a rather large whisky and soda, which she had allowed in the spirit of encouragement, he had become rather listless and drooping eyelids suggested that he was better off in bed, Elizabeth carrying on with the packing on her own.

By contrast, Lucia was feeling apprehensive. She had managed to convince Georgie that a move to Willows End was in both their interests but small self-doubts were beginning to surface, especially the prospect of having to stay at Grebe for several months. Mallards was such a fine house. She had spent a considerable amount of time and effort, not to mention great expense over the years, improving the fabric since its purchase from Mapp. It had both character and charm. And now she was virtually giving it away, she reflected, to someone who seemed to possess neither.

Georgie had wrapped his collection of bibelots in mountains of tissue paper and was now transferring boxes from his sitting-room on to the landing.
'Box number one contains my silver snuff boxes and Vesta cases. My porcelain Greek mythology figures are in box number two.'

Foljambe was stood alongside him, notebook in hand and was writing everything down furiously as Georgie spoke.

'Now did I put my scrimshaw in that box? Oh, how tar'some! I'll have to check it again,' and he knelt down and began to carefully unpack and unravel its contents.

Two removal lorries arrived – Jensen pantechnicons that could easily swallow up the entire contents of Mallards House. The first was to transport essential items to Grebe and the second would take the majority of the heavy furniture to a storage facility at East Guldeford. In turn, it would be brought to Willows End.

Grosvenor let in the removal men. There were four of them, a thick-set man with greying hair named Mr. Brocklehurst, firmly in charge.

'Sir George would like you to start with the upstairs rooms first,' she told them. 'Everything has been put into boxes. Lady Pillson has marked 'Grebe' on the ones that are going there and all the rest need to go into storage.'

The two younger removal men gave each other a knowing glance as they heard 'Sir George' and 'Lady Pillson' being mentioned, each contemplating a handsome tip at the end of the job.

'Right you are, ma'am,' replied Mr. Brocklehurst, 'But first of all... are you making a cup of tea? Thirsty work all this removing!'

Half an hour later, for several cups were drunk and numerous Digestives dunked, boxes began to leave Mallards. Lucia and Georgie sat in the garden-room, watching proceedings through the open door. Georgie marvelled at how agile and nimble the removal men appeared to be, despite their large frames. Lucia moved to the piano. She had reluctantly decided not to take it to Grebe, where the damper air might cause it some lasting damage.

'Georgie, *un po di musica*? One last time?'

Georgie, relieved to be doing something active, nodded his head and moved to sit alongside Lucia. A book of Diabelli duets, recently purchased, lay open on the music desk.

'*Primo* or *secondo*, Georgie?' asked Lucia.

Having heard her practicing the upper part the previous week, he graciously insisted on attempting the lower.

'*Uno, due, tre…*' and the music began.

Lost in the sonorous world of Diabelli, twenty minutes had flown by by the time Mr. Brocklehurst entered the room.

'Sorry to interrupt your Lordship, but we needs to start clearing this room.'

'Of course. Do start,' replied Georgie, adding 'Diabelli, you know,' as the removal man began to unscrew the rear leg of the piano. Lucia and Georgie returned to the sofa and sat transfixed as the entire contents of the room slowly disappeared. They stood up and moved to the garden as the sofa was eventually carried out.

Not having quite the same volume of contents to move, the Mapp-Flint removal van was already packed and ready for its rickety journey into Tilling. Empty of its contents,

Grebe looked even more tired and drab than Elizabeth had previously noticed. Not only that, but a rather cavalier move on the part of the two young removal men had left a nasty scrape on the hall wallpaper.

Mapp and the Major stood on the front steps.

'Sorry to leave, Liz-girl?' asked the Major.

'Not at all, Benjy. Grebe has been a millstone around our necks. No wonder Lucia foisted it off on me.'

'And no more long walks into Tilling,' continued the Major, who had begun to find the distance a little taxing recently.

Locking the front door for the last time, the Mapp-Flints then squeezed themselves into the front of the aging Bedford, ready for the journey to Mallards.

As the Bedford met the Jenson, closely followed by the Rolls-Royce, mid-way between Mallards and Grebe, there was a brief hiatus, both drivers determined not to give way on the narrow road. It was Mapp who suggested they pull over to the side and she waved enthusiastically as a gloomy looking Lucia passed by.

Five minutes later, both couples were to be found inside their new abodes, inspecting the internal fabric for anything untoward. Mallards was, of course, in pristine condition. Lucia had had most of the house redecorated just a year or so before and had paid a handsome sum for new downstairs carpeting. Mapp beamed. Everything was smelling of roses.

As she surveyed the the large gash in the wallpaper in the hall, the only thing Lucia could smell was the damp, not overpowering but noticeably disagreeable all the same. Georgie had already pointed out the terrible state of the flooring and the peeling decor.

'To be quite honest, Lucia,' said Georgie, 'I really don't think that I can stay here. I'm reminded of the Augean stables!'

'Nonsense, Georgie! This is no Herculean task! Grosvenor will have the place gleaming in no time at all. And remember that this is only a temporary measure. Mr. Maufe has promised that Willows End will be ready soon.'

'Living here might bring on my asthma again,' continued Georgie and he gave a pathetic little cough. 'And I shall worry about flooding. You know what happened before, Lucia!'

Memories of an upturned kitchen table bobbing along on the sea and several months spent on a fishing trawler with Mapp and an Italian Captain came flooding back to Lucia. Surviving against all the odds, they had returned back to a shocked Tilling, having been presumed drowned.

Grosvenor appeared, flustered.

'Beg your parden, ma'am, but there seems to be a problem in the kitchen – a terrible smell, if you don't mind me saying, sir.'

Lucia and Georgie accompanied by Mr. Brocklehurst made their way there, immediately noticing the unpleasant odour as soon as they entered.

'Drains. Georgie!' exclaimed Lucia.

'Oh, how could Mapp leave Grebe in such a state, Lucia?' asked Georgie as he gingerly opened the cupboard directly below the sink. The Major's shoddy repair work had not lasted and foul water was seeping from the pipes into the cupboard.

'That does look bad, your Lordship,' said Mr. Brocklehurst, 'Health hazard, I'd say!'

'There might be rats too, Lucia,' added Georgie. 'Big, fat, carnivorous ones!'

Lucia shuddered at the thought but she was determined not to be beaten.

'Highly unlikely, Georgie. Now let's start unpacking some boxes. Grosvenor can prepare some sandwiches. I'm sure Mr. Brocklehurst and his men have built up a hunger.'

Georgie picked up a box that had been brought in from the removal van. Fortunately it was not too heavy and he carried it up the stairs and into the main bedroom. It was not until he was leaving the room that he glanced upwards and saw the gaping hole in the ceiling.

'My goodness!' he exclaimed and shouted down the stairs for Lucia to view the damage.

Lucia surveyed the ceiling, sighing heavily.

'I had expected Elizabeth to make good the damage. I can't sleep in here, Georgie. I will have to have your room and you will have to sleep in the box room.'

'But that is tiny, Lucia! Where will I put my bibelots?'

Lucia gave Georgie a look – the kind of look that Georgie always tried to avoid.

'We could, Georgie… share a bedroom.'

Georgie emitted a noise that sounded like a cross between

a cough and a choke.

'Well, I suppose the box room will do – just for the moment.'

'That appears to be settled then, Georgie.'

Several hours later, the removal men had finished their task and were rewarded with a handsome tip from Georgie, Grosvenor handing them a large package of left-over sandwiches wrapped up in greaseproof paper as they left. Mr. Brocklehurst gave Grosvenor a wink as he said goodbye.

'If you're ever near East Guldeford, ma'am…'

Lucia had made a list. She would contact the builder, the decorator, the plumber and, just as a precaution, the ratcatcher the next day as a matter of urgency.

Chapter 15

'Well, that didn't take long!' exclaimed Georgie as he entered the garden-room after returning from the High Street one morning.

'What dear?' replied Lucia, sat on a sofa, a pile of papers by her side.

'The Major was nailing a large sign to the fence by Mallards – 'See the Roman Ruins and Discover the Legend of the Aureus'.

'Legend?'

'Legend indeed, Lucia! More like absolute fiction! Anyway, the Major insisted that everything would be ready for the first visitors this weekend. By the way, Mapp's charging two shillings for entrance.'

'So my dear friends could not resist mentioning my aborted idea to Elizabeth. Exactly as I predicted, Georgie.'

'And getting in on the act themselves, Lucia! Mr. Wyse has contributed several essays chronicling Roman life for the tour guide, Quaint Irene has been commissioned to paint a Roman mural on the potting shed and Diva is contracted to supply cakes and pastries for the tourists.'

'How delightful! We must attend the first tour. I'm sure dear Elizabeth will appreciate our interest,' and she returned to her papers.

In the garden at Mallards, Quaint Irene was administering the final touches to her Roman painting, depicting Gladitorial combat at the Colosseum. A pot of gold paint in her hand, she was now adding a touch of opulence to the scene which was, in truth, more Hollywood than ancient Rome.

'Splendid, Miss Coles!' exclaimed the Major, who had just returned from the Links.

'Isn't it wonderful , Benjy,' continued Mapp who was striding across the lawn, a basket of freshly-picked peas from the vegetable garden in her hand.

'Tilling is so fortunate to have its very own Michelangelo!'

'No need to flatter, Mapp. This is hardly the Sistine Chapel, you know,' replied Irene.

'Indeed, Quaint one.'

Withers appeared.

'Mrs. Plaistow to see you ma'am. She says it's urgent. She's waiting in the kitchen.'

Mapp was greeted by an excited Diva carrying a large tray, the contents of which were covered by tin foil.

'Janet has been experimenting, Elizabeth,' said Diva, almost out of breath and she removed the foil ceremoniously to reveal what appeared to be a veritable Roman feast.

'She went to the library and found a book all about the Roman diet and once she had tried one recipe she had to try them all!'

Mapp looked in astonishment at the weird and wonderful array of food.

'Diva, dear. So delighted that you have risen to the challenge, as it were, but jam puffs and fruit scones are more what I had in mind.'

'Not a stuffed mouse or a braised thrush?' indicating the

poor, unfortunate creatures as they lay, almost barely recognisable, on the tray.

'Most definitely not, Diva!' replied Mapp, horrified.

'They're quite fresh. The cat caught them both yesterday. Just try one of these, Elizabeth,' and she passed Mapp what appeared to be a small mushroom tartlet. Not wishing to offend Diva too much, Mapp bit into it with gusto and began to chew.

'Snails… from the garden.'

Mapp recoiled in horror and would have spat out the contents of her mouth there and then if she had not accidentally swallowed them, such was the shock. She rushed to the sink, found the nearest empty container, a larger gravy boat, filled it with water and downed the whole lot.

'Jam puffs and fruit scones it is then, Elizabeth. Au reservoir!' and she left, rather deflated.

In his study at Starling Cottage, Algernon Wyse was adding the finishing touches to his essay on 'Everyday Roman Life' to be featured in the tour guide each visitor would receive on entering the gardens at Mallards. He had also written an exhuberant piece entitled 'The Legend of the Aureus'. Mapp had finally persuaded Mr. Wyse to omit any references to the 'Pillson Aureus' but he had flatly refused to re-name it after the Mapp-Flints.

'I must take this to the printers, Susan,' he called upstairs to his wife. 'I will take the Royce,' for the printworks were on the outskirts of Tilling.

The printer had also been asked to print two hundred flyers, advertising the Roman Ruins, which were to be distributed to local shops and hotels. Elizabeth had designed this herself and featured the photograph of the unveiling of the aureus at the British Museum, minus Lucia and Georgie, the victims of a sharp pair of scissors. Visitors were encouraged to visit the 'ancestral' home of the Mapp-Flints, where 'some of the greatest antiquities since the discovery of Tutankhamun's tomb had been found'.

The Mapp-Flints were up bright and early on the Saturday morning. Mr. Wyse's tour guides had been delivered the day before and were looking particularly colourful, displayed on a large table in a fan arrangement. Being far more impressive and informative than she had expected, Mapp had now decided to charge sixpence for them and a large sign indicated that fact. The tour would consist of a talk from Mapp herself, by the entrance of the garden, a walk around the garden, where various pieces of pottery had been carefully positioned, Benjy leading the way and a visit to the potting shed (renamed The Roman Vault) which housed various tools (used for the excavations), some old books on Roman Britain and what could have been mistaken for an old and rather battered dustbin lid, though it had been labelled in Mapp's very own hand as 'Roman Shield – date unknown'. Visitors would then be treated to a cup of tea with either a jam puff or fruit scone, which they would consume in the *giardino segreto*. Mapp didn't really want visitors there but it was, at least, better than inviting them into the house itself. Those with larger appetites could then purchase further refreshments, swelling the coffers even more. There were no contingency plans, however, should it rain.

Mapp had found a box of broken pottery in the greenhouse soon after moving back to Mallards. She was not to know that Lucia had left it there entirely on purpose. Although the various pots, bowls and vases seemed ancient enough, there was no certainty that they were actually Roman in origin. However, there was nothing in particular to suggest that they *weren't* – and that was good enough for Mapp. She had placed the broken pieces amongst the flower beds at regular intervals, 'Please do not touch' signs by each one.

Diva arrived with two large tins containing the scones and jam puffs.

'Do you need any help, Elizabeth?' she asked. 'I can stay for an hour or two.'

'Diva, dear. Such kindness! Perhaps you could carry out the teacups and plates to the *giardino segreto*. Withers was going to do it but I've had to send her on a little errand. Benjy was supposed to order extra milk from the milkman this morning for the teas but completely forgot. Withers is now getting ten extra pints from Twistevant's.'

'Ten pints, Elizabeth?'

'Yes, dear. Ten pints. Anything wrong?'

'Are you expecting a very large crowd? Ten pints does seem rather a lot of milk. Sometimes I use less than that in a whole week!'

'Ten pints, dear. Now do be careful with the crockery.'

The first tour had been advertised at ten thirty and by that time a small gathering had formed by the 'Queue Here' sign, helpfully installed by the Major. At the front were the Padre and Evie, the Wyses followed by Lucia and Georgie. Unfortunately, Quaint Irene had been forced to stay at home to nurse her maid Lucy who had contracted chickenpox, or so the doctor thought. A family with a dog, an elderly couple and a man wearing a raincoat and thick-lensed spectacles completed the crowd.

Mapp surveyed the waiting group from the garden-room. It was now nearly quarter to eleven and she could not wait any longer. Perhaps more people would come along to the afternoon tour. She opened the front door and stepped outside.

'Greetings everyone and welcome to The Roman Ruins at Mallards – home of the legendary aureus. Now do come this way. Major Mapp-Flint will issue you with a ticket.'

The queue obediently filed past the Major as he affably divested each visitor of two shillings. Only Lucia and Mr. Wyse purchased a tour guide.

Mapp read from a small card which she held infront of her.'

'Can we imagine what it would have been like to stand here, on this very spot, nearly two thousand years ago, when Julius Caesar first invaded Britain?

Today you are treading in the footsteps of those first Romans who made their way to Tilling…'

'When will she stop?' whispered Georgie to Lucia, ten

minutes into her speech. 'She's managing the impossible – to talk a great deal but say very little!'

'Don't be cruel, Georgie. At least some of it makes sense!'

'Yes, the bit at the beginning, penned by Mr. Wyse, I presume.'

'Georgie!'

Once finished, Mapp did not invite questions but merely handed the reins to the Major who asked all the visitors politely to follow behind as he trailed around the garden, pointing at various objects, half-hidden amongst the shrubbery.

'What's that?' asked a small boy, indicating an upturned bowl, rustic-red in colour.

'That, my boy, is an ancient Roman blood-letting vessel. The Roman doctor would get his knife and….'

'Thank you, Major,' called Mapp from the back of the line, impressed by the Major's quick response but worried that his explanation might be too gruesome for a young boy. 'We can answer questions at the end of the tour.'

'Right you are, Elizabeth. Carry on marching,' and the tramp around the flower beds continued.

'Our Roman Vault,' announced Mapp proudly, 'And please do take some time to admire the wonderful mural painted by Tilling's own Irene Coles of Royal Academy fame.

The crowd filed into the potting shed, had a quick look around and promptly filed out again. The man wearing the raincoat, however, began to inspect the display of tools, picking up a rather severe-looking hand pick.

'Do put that down, sir,' said a somewhat concerned Mapp. 'All the exhibits are very fragile.'

'Mother had one of these,' replied the man.

'Really? Was she an archaeologist?'

'No. She was a misandrist, actually. Poor father!' and the man looked at the pick, 'This was the last thing he ever saw!'

Mapp wasn't sure what a misandrist was, but it didn't sound very good and she ushered the man out of the shed.

By now, most people were drinking tea and eating Diva's baking in the *giardino segreto*. The small boy was trying to find the Major, in order to hear the rest of his explanation, but the Major had ventured inside Mallards for something a little stronger than tea. Lucia strode across the lawn to speak to Mapp.

'Elizabeth, dear! Such an enjoyable talk. One or two factual innaccuracies, I think, but quite riveting all the same.'

Mapp ignored the delicate rebuke.

'So glad that you could be one of the first visitors, Lucia. Did you enjoy the tour Sir George?'

Georgie, a large jam puff in his mouth, nodded enthusiastically.

'The flower beds seem to have yielded a veritable treasure trove of Roman pottery, Elizabeth.'

Mapp began to colour as she began to think of a convincing reply.

'I managed to coax dear old Coplen out of retirement to tidy up the garden and, such was his enthusiasm, his spade reached depths never plundered before. Dear Coplen, quite overwhelmed he was when I informed him of the importance of his find.'

'Surprising to hear that, Elizabeth. Coplen could hardly lift a spade the last time he worked for me. That is why I had to dismiss him.'

At that point the Major came running out of the house.

'Guess what, Liz-girl?' he said, excitedly.

'Whatever is the matter, Benjy?'

'Just had a phone call. The Peasmarsh Womens' Institute have just had their afternoon trip to the gardens at Brickwell House cancelled and wondered if they might come here instead.'

'How many, Benjy?'

'Thirty-two ladies, plus the driver of the coach.'

A grin appeared on Mapp's face as she quickly calculated the possible afternoon profits.

'Send Withers to Wasters to pick up some more fruit scones and jam puffs, Benjy. Please excuse me Lucia, Sir George,' and she ran back into the house.

'Quick, Georgie, we'll make a swift exit,' whispered Lucia as she saw the man in the raincoat and thick-lensed glasses approach them. Bidding 'Au reservoir' to Mr. Wyse, Susan, the Padre and Evie, they made their way out of the garden and onto the High Street.

Chapter 16

It was Thursday morning. Diva picked up the post which had just fallen through her letterbox. She held two neatly typed envelopes. Diva opened the larger one first. It read:

Dear Diva,
You are invited to Grebe for an evening of poetry and literature to be followed by Debussy and dinner this Saturday. Cadman will run you home afterwards…

Evie took the post to the Rev'd Bartlett who was in his study adding the finishing touches to his sermon for the following Sunday.

'Two letters, Kenneth,' squeaked Evie, placing them on his desk. He opened the smaller of the two. It read:

Dear Padre and Evie,
You are both invited to Mallards for a SURPRISE evening of entertainment to be followed by dinner this Saturday…

Susan Wyse had opened both letters that had been delivered to Starling Cottage that morning.

'Algernon, we have been invited to Grebe on Saturday for one of Lucia's literary and musical evenings.'

'Splendid!' replied Mr. Wyse, 'I had wondered when the Pillsons would start entertaining again.'

'A slight problem, Algernon.'

'Yes?'

'The Mapp-Flints have also invited us for dinner on the same evening. They are promising a surprise evening of entertainment.'

Susan passed her husband the invitation. He looked at it amusedly.

'Capital! I do like surprises!'

Lucia was already planning the said evening, with suggestions by Georgie gratefully received but quietly sidelined.

'Dante, Georgie, for starters, followed perhaps by a little Byron and…' she hesitated, 'Virginia Woolf?'

Lucia had just finished reading *To The Lighthouse* and felt it to be of enough literary merit to warrant her interest, even though she had found it rather bewildering.

'Isn't that a little too highbrow?' said Georgie. 'What about that rather racy novel *Love in a Cold Climate* by Nancy Mitford?'

Lucia's face began to colour.

'I'm afraid I don't know that one, Georgie.'

'Oh, I thought I saw it under your pillow at the hospital. Must have been mistaken! Is that the post?'

Meanwhile, a small green van made its way along Tilling High Street 'T & G Electricals, Hastings' emblazoned on its side in bright orange. It pulled up just outside Mallards and two men, in smart uniform, emerged from the vehicle. Moving to the back of the van, they opened the rear doors and very carefully removed a large, heavy rectangular box. Mapp had been on the lookout for the men since mid-morning and had instructed Withers to

130

open the front door, ready for their arrival at the front steps.

'Where's it going ma'am?' asked the elder of the two gentlemen.

'In that room there – in the far corner, please,' replied Mapp 'And do be careful!'

'Right you are ma'am,' replied the younger man and they expertly unpacked and installed the contents of the box – soon to be Mapp's pride and joy.

After a brief demonstration, the gentleman left and Mapp turned her attention to more pressing matters, for she had also received an envelope from Grebe.

'Typical of Lucia to choose *our* night for her little evening, Benjy. And more Debussy! Do you remember when she vamped her way through some dirge called *La Mer*? I felt positively queasy during the whole performance.'

Benjy nodded, though he had no recollection of either the music or the evening itself.

'The trouble with that kind of music, Benjy, is that it is already so crammed with wrong notes that Lucia feels at liberty to add some more of her own, with hideous consequences!'

'Absolutely, Elizabeth. My ears were assaulted too!'

'Really, Benjy?' and she gave him a loving smile. 'We are a pair, aren't we? Quite suited! Now what shall I do about this letter?'

'Just hold your horses, old girl! See what replies *we* get first.'

Georgie had read the letter from the Mapp-Flints with indignation, passing it on to Lucia with a sigh.

'Typical of Mapp to choose *our* night for her *surprise* evening – whatever that may be, Lucia! What are you going to do?'

Lucia closed her eyes and breathed in deeply. She then moved to the piano and began to rummage through a pile of sheet music on the lid, as if nothing was of concern.

'Well, Lucia?'

'Simply an unfortunate clash of dates, Georgie. I'll send Cadman round with notes saying that... that Foljambe has just knocked over a vase on the piano, the water has seeped into the mechanism and it can't be played for the next two weeks meaning that we will have to postpone the evening.'

'Foljambe?'

'Grosvenor, if you like, Georgie!'

'I really can't believe it, Lucia! You're giving in to Mapp?'

'We can't risk aggravating her just yet, Georgie. In any case, I'm rather curious as to the surprise she has in store. Aren't you?'

'Well, I suppose so and it does give us a little more time to practice the Debussy duet,' added Georgie.

Chapter 17

The Rolls drew up alongside Mallards. Cadman opened up the door for Lucia and Georgie.

'Pick up at eleven, ma'am?' asked Cadman.

'Thank you, Cadman,' replied Lucia as she stepped out of the car. Withers opened the front door and welcomed the latest arrivals, the Wyses, the Bartletts, Diva and Quaint Irene having already been admitted.

'Lulu, how lovely to see you and Sir George,' effused Mapp and she mock-curtseyed to Georgie, 'Welcome to my dear Mallards!'

Lucia quickly surveyed the room. Some of the considerable surplus profit from the house sale had been invested in new furniture and Lucia had to admit to herself that the house was looking splendid. The only exception to this was the large array of pictures on the walls – Mapp's very own creations.

'Such delightful pictures, Elizabeth.'

'Oh, just my own little daubs, Lucia.'

'Such an original style. Quite…' Lucia searched for the word, 'Unique.'

'Not the word I'd use Lucia!' chipped in Quaint Irene.

Mapp awaited further opinion from Irene but, thankfully, nothing was forthcoming. Turning to Georgie, she offered high praise.

'Of course, my little piccies cannot compare with your *oeuvre*, Sir George.'

'Oh, do call me Georgie! Sir George is terribly formal.'

Although Georgie's artistic skills were well-considered in Tilling, wider recognition was still to come.

'Actually,' said Lucia, addressing the whole room, 'Sir George… er, Georgie has been asked to become a Trustee of the National Gallery. He has also kindly donated several of his pictures.'

There was a gentle ripple of applause at this news. Georgie gave Lucia a glance, just catching her eye. Yes, he had been approached by the Board of the Gallery and he may have joked about giving them one of his pictures, but Lucia was, once again, overstepping the mark, gilding the lily, if indeed there was one to gild.

'Put in a good word for me!' joked Irene.

As drinks were passed around by Withers, the general chit-chat could not disguise the air of expectation and anticipation at the proposed surprise. At last, unable to feign indifference anymore, Susan Wyse spoke up.

'Dear Elizabeth, I do believe you have a little surprise in store for us all. Will this be revealed before or after dinner?

Mapp looked at the clock on the mantelpiece. It was fast approaching eight.

'Dear ones,' she replied 'The surprise is just about to start. Do come along,' and she made her way out of the garden-room, the rest following, Pied Piper fashion.

The guests were lead to a medium-sized room that had once been used as an additional study when Lucia had been Mayor of Tilling. The room was entirely empty apart from two rows of chairs facing what appeared to be a large box covered by a shocking-pink damask curtain.

'Do find a chair, everybody,' trilled Mapp as the guests filed into the room. Lucia and Georgie, being the last to enter, found themselves sat on two striped deck-chairs that had been recently requisitioned from the garden shed, Mapp having run out of more comfortable recliners.

Mapp addressed her seated guests, Major Benjy obediently stood by her side.

'My dear friends – your surprise!' and she ceremoniously pulled the cover off the box to reveal a Pye LV30C television set, featuring the latest nine inch screen. There was a gasp from Susan, a hoot from Irene and then a collective round of applause as Mapp beamed at her audience.

Television broadcasting was still in its infancy and the Mapp-Flint television set was one of only a handful in Tilling and the surrounding area. Although owning one was the preserve of the wealthy, most of those rich enough to afford one actually preferred the radio, finding the visual element rather vulgar. Nevertheless, Mapp was keen to demonstate her new-found wealth and there was no doubt that having one would generate a fair degree of excitement amongst her friends.

Mapp then signalled to the Major who retrieved an unwieldy and rather dangerous-looking indoor aerial from behind the television, standing it on top of a stool that was in the opposite corner of the room. Mapp switched on the appliance and the glass screen gradually flickered into life, a fuzzy picture appearing, though rather indistinct.

'Just move the stool a little, Benjy,' Mapp called and the Major moved it firstly to the left (no improvement), then to the right (even worse) and finally lifted it up to shoulder height. This resulted in the picture becoming stable and much clearer. Mapp turned up the volume and a tinny voice could be heard announcing the start of *Café Continental,* broadcast live from the BBC studios at Alexandra Palace.

The Major, forced to continue holding the stool aloft, was unable to watch the programme from where he stood but the rest of the guests, including Lucia, were positively mesmerised by the tiny screen as it relayed the popular variety show directly into Mallards House. Tonight's programme, hosted by the Maitre d'hôtel, Claude Frederic, featured a performing dogs act from Romania, a magician who miraculously managed to chop himself in half, a children's chorus from Pimlico and the internationally renowned zither player, Anton Karas, playing his *Harry Lime Theme* from *The Third Man.* Jaques Laroque and his L'Orchestra Pigalle closed the programme with a spirited performance of melodies by Rogers and Hart.

'Bravo!' shouted Mr. Wyse as the broadcast ended.
'Spendid performance!' added Susan.

'What fun!' was Diva's contribution and Quaint Irene, who had resolved to hate the experience had to admit to herself that she would willingly return for more.

Georgie turned to Lucia.

'Well, I quite enjoyed that. How about you, Lucia?

Lucia, addressing her reply to the whole room, was initially effusive in her praise.

'Quite marvellous, dear Elizabeth. A modern miracle, indeed. Though…' she added, 'Not quite a substitute for live entertainment... and such a small screen.'

'You must bring your glasses next time, Lucia,' replied Mapp, to the amusement of the others, even Georgie, 'Though my dear Benjy has just ordered a large magnifying lens. He saw one advertised in the paper.'

'Filled with water, you know. Sits infront of the television. Just need to top it up now and again,' added the Major.

'Just like you then Benjy-boy!' remarked Quaint Irene.

'It will just be like going to the pictures!' exclaimed Diva.

'Then I will have to start charging a shilling entrance, dear Godiva!' replied Mapp.

Mapp's dining table looked luxuriant with a central display of garden flowers from the *giardino segreto*. She had gone to the trouble of writing place cards for each guest and several menus, neatly typed, were stood on the table at regular intervals.

Starter
Moules de Mallards
Main
Beef Wellington

137

Dessert
Peach Melba

The guests looked appreciatively at the menus. It was clear that Mapp's dinner parties were going to be much more enjoyable affairs from now on.

'Moules de Mallards?' enquired Lucia as Withers poured her a glass of Chateau Saint-Estèphe.

'Yes, my own secret recipe to celebrate moving back home, Lucia.'

Lucia's mind was cast back to the time when Mapp had discovered her own secret recipe for *Lobster à la Riseholme* one Boxing Day – the day of the great flood. She was about to make a cutting comment but managed to stop herself. Any discussions about secrets were best avoided.

Lucia had hoped that the *Moules de Mallards* would be tasteless and rubbery but, in truth, they were succulent and sweet, a hint of spice just detectable in the accompanying liquer. The *Beef Wellington* did full justice to the formidable Duke and the dessert was a triumph of both artistry and taste.

'A sheer delight!' pronounced Mr. Wyse after his last spoonful of ice-cream, coated with a sharp raspberry sauce, was devoured. 'My compliments to to the hostess,' and he bowed his head towards Mapp, 'And host, of course,' bowing again, in the direction of the Major.

'Yes, it was rather delicious, Mapp,' enthused Diva, Quaint Irene agreeing.

'Lang may yer lum reek, Mistress Mapp!' added the Padre, wiping his mouth with his napkin.

Everyone assumed that this was a positive comment. 'Withers will be bringing coffee in soon. Might I suggest a quick rubber?'

There was a look of panic as Mapp made this suggestion. The Mapp-Flint's bridge-playing status had still to be resolved by the Tilling Bridge Club, following the discovery of their cheating at the bridge tournament. Then everybody looked at Lucia, a move which Lucia interpreted as the masses pleading for guidance.

'A quick rubber would be...' began Lucia, pausing very dramatically as the rest of the room waited eagerly for the close of the sentence, 'A splendid way to end the evening.'

'Absolutely!' added Georgie, 'Splendid!'

'I'll get the cards,' said the Major, relieved.

All past animosities seemed to dissipate in the following hour as each couple chatted, joked, laughed and reminisced about times past. Mapp was buoyant, knowing that the evening had been a triumph and Lucia, though slightly envious, had enjoyed the entertainment, the food and the company of all her friends.

Cadman arrived at the appointed hour and, after saying their goodbyes and thankyous, Lucia and Georgie made their way back to Grebe. The journey from Mallards to Grebe seemed slightly longer now.

On entering, Lucia sensed the rather cold atmosphere, in complete contrast to the warm and convivial one

Mallards had had. Thoughts turned to Willows End which was almost ready for her and Georgie's arrival – though the word 'soon' appeared to have a different meaning in architectural speak.

'We will have a Grand Ball, Georgie,' said Lucia, as Georgie removed his coat and hat. He gave her a quizzical look.

'At Willows End, Georgie. It will be the highlight of the social calendar in East Sussex,' and her mind began to race as she pondered the infinite possibilities.

'A string quartet, Georgie?'

'How about a whole orchestra, Lucia?' replied Georgie, a hint of sarcasam in his answer.

'Good idea, Georgie. Speak to your colleagues at the Covent Garden Opera Company would you? They've got a pretty good band. I must remember to invite dear Noël. And we must have a wonderful spread – something a little different, perhaps. *Harper's* has some wonderful recipes by Elizabeth David. I'll find out her telephone number and give her a call,' and she moved to her desk and began scribbling down a long list of names and exotic fruits and vegetables.

'L-Y-C-H-E or double E, Georgie?

Bewildered, Georgie shook his head and retired upstairs.

Chapter 18

Having spent a busy three weeks moving into Willows End, Lucia spent the following week finishing off preparations for the Grand Ball. Georgie had already secured the services of a small ensemble of orchestral players from Covent Garden and Elizabeth David had been kind enough to agree to manage the food preparations for the evening. Lucia had spoken to her several times on the telephone and was looking forward to meeting her on the day of the ball, when she had agreed to arrive in the early morning to oversee the kitchen. Additional tables and chairs had been procured from the Church hall – a generous donation to Church funds having been made.

Lucia had sent out invitations to around fifty guests and had received replies from most of them. The list consisted of a mixture of old money, new money and some notable individuals whose names were instantly recognisable – Noël Coward (of course), John Gielgud and the stars of Georgie's favourite film *Brief Encounter*, Trevor Howard and Celia Johnson. They had both agreed to attend the ball on learning that Noël was a 'dear and close' friend of the hostess. Lucia decided not to tell Georgie that she had invited them – it would be a lovely surprise for him.

Sat at her desk, Lucia was adding the finishing touches to the menu. Mrs. David had suggested that cold starters and desserts could be prepared in advance with just the main course to worry about on the evening itself. Lucia's list of exotic fruits had made their way into a fruit salad of mind-boggling complexity and kohlrabi, purple sweet potatoes, salsify and romanescu would accompany a venison ragout. Between them, Mr. Twistevant and Mr. Twemlow, the grocer, assured Lucia that they would be able to procure the said fruits and vegetables – but at a premium price. The starter would be a relatively simple egg mayonnaise, Georgie's one and only suggestion which Lucia thought she had better embrace wholeheartedly.

'Anything left for me to do, Lucia?' enquired Georgie, who was at a loose end, his rooms now in order, his bibelots polished and on display and having just finished crocheting a new set of six egg cosies, the previous ones in use now old and worn. Georgie himself felt neither old nor worn. The move to Willows End had gone relatively smoothly and he was enjoying the extra space, the air of tranquility and the excitement of the upcoming ball.

'Not especially, Georgie. Though you might ask the Padre if he has remembered to stack the tables and chairs. Oh, you could ring the florist and check whether she has everything in order. And…' she added, 'Remind Foljame to provide me with the list of additional staff,' for Lucia had asked her to organise some extra help for the evening.

'I have the list already, Lucia. Foljambe gave it to me yesterday.'

Lucia was just about to say that Foljambe had strict instructions to pass the list directly to her but bit her lip before any invective could be issued. Any criticism of Foljambe was tantamount almost to an attack on Georgie – or so *he* felt.

The Mapp-Flints had just returned from a week-end in Brighton, where Elizabeth had met an old school chum, recently widowed, who was now looking forward to happier days. Whilst Mapp had spent two afternoons chatting merrily with her friend, Benjy had taken advantage of the local hostelries with the full blessing of his wife. The Major had developed an annoying habit of falling to sleep mid-afternoon and Mapp did not wish to subject her friend to any of Benjy's snoring.

On his travels, the Major had visited the seafront penny arcades, played 'Housey Housey' and made a respectable profit of ten shillings. He had then invested the said winnings on an odds-on favourite running at Haydock at two o' clock. Benjy had arrived back at their hotel rather disappointed, slightly tipsy and penniless.

The Major was now perusing the *Radio Times* and planning his evening schedule. The Mapp-Flints were making the most of their Pye LV30C. The Major never missed the *Television Newsreel* which had now replaced the morning newspaper as his chief source of news. Mapp enjoyed *Come Dancing* with its colourful costumes (well, she assumed they were colourful) and imaginative choreography. Mapp also allowed the Major to watch the races as long as he remained a passive viewer.

There was a call from upstairs.

'Benjy, you can come and look now,' trilled Mapp.

'Right away, Liz-girl,' and he strode up the stairs to the bedroom where Elizabeth was wearing her new gown made of bright orange silk, procured from Hanningtons in Brighton.

'Well? What do you think?'

The Major was staring intensely at the dress. Mapp was not sure whether this was a good or a bad sign.

'It's so….so….orange!'

'Of course it is, Benjy. But do you like it?'

The Major now had two possible courses of action. He could either tell the truth and ruin the rest of the day or even the whole week, or he could lie through his teeth and keep his wife happy.

'You will be the belle of the ball, Elizabeth,' he replied.

'And you will be my handsome prince, Benjy!'

Evie Bartlett sat at her sewing machine, sewing the hem of her ball dress. This had been constructed from several surplus surplices, a disused altar cloth with trimmings from a box of secondhand clothes that had remained unsold at the recent Church jumble sale. Evie had been working on her dress ever since the invitation to the ball had been received as her pleading to be allowed to spend just a small amount on a new gown had fallen on deaf ears. The Padre was not against frivolity itself – just the cost of it, especially if he had to pay for it himself.

Evie held the dress up. Never having attended a proper ball before, she was not sure whether her efforts would cut the mustard, but it looked fine in her eyes. There was little point in asking Kenneth for his opinion – a man whose wardrobe consisted primarily of white shirts, grey jackets and slacks. He had no discernable views on fashion whatsoever.

The Bartletts had been the only couple to visit Willows End before the date of the ball. At Church, the Padre had suggested to Lucia and Georgie that he would be willing to conduct a house blessing. They has readily agreed, not realising that this would involve him sprinkling Holy water in every room at Willows End, whilst reciting the appropriate prayers. After the ceremony, Lucia had asked Evie how often the Padre had performed this service. She, rather reluctantly, replied that this was his first one, suggesting to Lucia that the Reverend Bartlett was using his ecclesiastical duties to mask his inherent nosiness.

Evie put on the dress and checked herself in the mirror. It fitted a treat and she began to waltz around the room, imagining herself in her husband's arms as she hummed the waltz from *Die Fledermaus*.

Diva sat in her tea-shop alone, having sent Janet off on an errand. The last customer had left over half an hour ago and there was little prospect of any more paying guests appearing that day.

She was keen to learn whether her request for funds from The Lady Pillson Charitable Trust had been successful, but no such communication had been made and she was

145

reluctant to ask Lucia outright. Now that she was chief supplier of jam puffs and fruit scones for Elizabeth's tours, the need for a larger oven was increasingly apparent and she had sent off for a number of brochures detailing the latest designs. In moments of boredom she would read and re-read all about the benefits of modern electric kitchen appliances and wondered what Lucia's new kitchen at Willows End would be like.

Diva had expected an invitation to visit as soon as Lucia and Georgie had moved to their new house but none was forthcoming. Meeting Lucia whilst daily marketing in the High Street, Lucia had explained that Willows End, though habitable, was not quite ready for visitors yet as workmen were still seeing to the final touches. Indeed, she explained, Mr. Maufe had to 'sign off' the building.
'You won't have to wait long, dear,' Lucia had said tantalisingly.

Thrilled to receive an invitation to the ball – 'Such excitement in Tilling!' – Diva had telephoned her cousin, Alice, who lived in nearby High Halden. She was now retired but had been a seamstress since her early teens and occasionally made dresses and gowns for family and friends. Alice had an attic full of material, collected over many years and Diva had chosen a floral rayon crepe fabric which Alice thought had originally been on sale at Liberty's shop in London. A quick worker, Alice had measured Diva (would there be enough material?), cut the cloth (there was just enough!) and sewn up the garment in a matter of a few days. The dress now hung in the wardrobe, awaiting its debut.

Like Evie, Diva had never been to a ball before, though in her early married life she had been a regular dancer. Mr. Plaistow had mastered both the Viennese Waltz and the Foxtrot and the pair had even entered a dancing competition in Brighton one summer. Happy memories but sadly now fading with the passage of time.

Quaint Irene, rose in mouth, had been practising the Tango with Lucy – always a willing partner. Initially, when the invitation to the ball arrived on her doorstep, she had thrown it aside – not her kind of thing at all. However, she did not wish to upset Lucia as a refusal to attend might be seen as a snub. Therefore she had resolved to learn at least one dance and the Tango seemed the most apt for her disposition.

She was also desperately keen to see the interior of Willows End. A life-size mural might be just the thing to liven up a blank expanse of wall. In her mind's eye she saw both Lucia and Georgie – *au naturale* – embracing a large weeping willow, representing the present with a mallard and a grebe perched in its branches to represent the past.

A photograph of Miss Coles had recently appeared in the *Hampshire Argus*. Her painting entitled 'Bodily Quirks', which she had given to Mapp for the Hospital auction, had sold for an extraordinary amount. Indeed, Mapp had quipped that the final price was infinitely more shocking than the depicted figure itself. An American art collector staying in Hastings had, by chance, seen a leaflet advertising the sale and arrived by taxi just before the auction was due to start and was seen in animated conversation with Irene.

As 'Bodily Quirks' was held aloft, Lucia felt it was both her moral and civic duty to start the bidding. It soon became apparent that there was a genuine interest being shown in the work and Lucia kept on increasing her bid.

'Lucia!' Georgie had whispered, 'Just be careful, or you might end up with it!'

'The secret, Georgie,' she replied, 'Is knowing when to stop. I don't think we're quite finished yet!'

There was a tense moment as the American failed to top Lucia's final bid.

'Going for three hundred and eighty pounds to Lady Pillson. Going... going...'

'Four hundred!' called out the American.

'Sold!' cried Lucia and the auctioneer brought down his gavel.

After paying, the American – a Mr. Irvine B. Waldings – had instructed the auctioneer to send the painting to the Walker Art Center in Minneapolis.

'You'll never guess where my painting's being sent to, Lucia,' said Irene, meeting Lucia after the auction. 'To Minneapolis!'

'The Walker Art Center, by any chance, Irene?' she replied.

'Gosh, Lucia – I didn't realise you knew all about the American art scene too. One of the most prestigious museums of modern art in the States.'

'Absolutely, dear.'

Lucia didn't really know very much about the art world across the Atlantic and had certainly never heard of the Walker Art Center. However, she had heard, very clearly, the conversation between Mr. Waldings and the auctioneer, just a few minutes previously.

Chapter 19

Lucia rose at five, Georgie a little later at six, both keen to attend to the list of jobs each one had made in order to prepare for the ball, that evening. Olga, who had arrived the night before (and the first to use one of the guest bedrooms at Willows End) slept until eleven.

Elizabeth David arrived bright and early, Lucia having sent Cadman to transport her to Willows End. After a brief greeting, she set to work straight away in the kitchen – now filled with exotic fruits and vegetables delivered by the High Street errand boys the previous evening, fresh meat brought by the butcher that morning and nine dozen eggs procurred at very reasonable cost from the farmer next door. The new Kelvinator refridgerator was similarly well-stocked.

Throughout the day, the ground floor of Willows End was gradually transformed. The tables and chairs from the Church hall were arranged to form a single large table sitting fifty guests in reasonable comfort, positioned to the left the central staircase. On the other side, a large space had been cleared for dancing, the band to perform on the steps of the straircase.

Georgie had just finished writing out the place cards in neat italic script using his new Conway Stewart that Lucia had given him as a moving in gift, as the crockery and cutlery were being set out. Lucia surveyed the scene –

everything looked splendid and the kitchen was operating smoothly under Mrs. David's command.

At five-thirty the musicians from the Covent Garden Opera Company arrived – an eight-piece ensemble consisting of strings and woodwind. 'No brass, Georgie!' had been Lucia's strict instructions. They set up their music stands, loaded them with copious amounts of sheet music and went off towards the kitchen, in search of liquid refreshment. Georgie had been assured that there was no need for them to rehearse beforehand.

Lucia signalled for Georgie to retire upstairs in order to dress for the ball. Foljambe had already laid out his dinner suit and jacket, his Insignia carefully placed alongside. In her room, Lucia opened the wardbrobe and stared at the gown she was about to wear. It was almost too beautiful to put on – a lilac taffeta creation by Norman Hartnell no less. Lucia – with just a quiet word to the right person – had managed to leapfrog his enormous waiting list and had attended three fittings at his studio in quick succession, where she had enjoyed Mr. Hartnell's personal attention.

Meeting briefly at the top of the staircase, they descended hand-in-hand, carefully avoiding the music stands, to a round of applause from Olga, the musicians and servants, just as the first cars began to arrive, dropping off their resplendant occupants at the front door of Willows End. Grosvenor stood alongside, holding a silver tray of sparkling flute glasses brimming with Veuve Clicquot-Ponsardin Champagne.

As with most big events, it began with small talk.
'So delighted you could come.'
'The band's from Covent Garden, actually.'
'Nothing special, dear. Just one of dear Norman's.'
'A three hour journey? How tar'some!'
'Elizabeth David. I've already given her several recipes.'
'Edward Maufe. Look, he's over there with Miss Bracely, checking the light switch.'
Olga, having recently visited the construction site of the new Festival Hall in London with Sir Malcom Sargent (who was already planning the first concerts), was amazed that Willows End had been built so quickly.
'Modern building techniques, Miss Bracely,' mused Mr. Maufe, 'We can achieve almost anything, these days. Willows End is the way forward and Lady Pillson must be congratulated for being so bold.'
'And when do you expect Guilford Cathedral to be finished?' asked Olga, rather cheekily.
'That, dear lady, is another matter entirely!'

A short while later, the Wyse's Royce, transporting the owners, Mapp-Flints and Diva arrived. The Padre and Evie were walking to Willows End and Quaint Irene intended to peddle for she was on no accounts wearing a ball gown – not even for Lucia!

Mr. Wyse strode up to Lucia.

'Lady Pillson, such an honour!' and he bowed in his customary fashion.

'And Sir George,' added Susan, her MBE proudly on display around her neck.

'Lulu darling!' exclaimed Mapp, embracing Lucia with the gusto one might embrace a lost child who had just been found. 'Sono così felice rivederti!' and she kissed Lucia on both cheeks, checking that she was in full view of the other guests. She then tripped off to join the throng that was gathering infront of the band, now playing *In the Shadows*.

Lucia was waiting for just one more car – that containing Noël Coward, John Gielgud, Trevor Howard and Celia Johnson. Earlier that month she had feared that they would be unable to attend the ball as Noël's new musical *Ace of Clubs* was having a shakey start in the provinces. However, with its London opening, things were more settled and critics slightly kinder.

She did not have long to wait before a dark green Bentley purred down the drive, the unmistakable face (unless you were Mapp, of course) of Noël Coward staring out of the front passenger window.

'Am I in Tilling, or Manhattan, Lucia darling?' he called. 'What a splendid building. The countryside is full of architectural surprises!' and he stepped out of the car.

'Why, thank you, Noël. Out with the old and in with the new, as they say. So pleased to see you all, Mr. Gielgud, Mr. Howard, Miss Johnson. My husband, Sir George, is such a fan. *Brief Encounter* is his favourite film. He will have such a surprise!'

Heads turned as Lucia's celebrity quartet made their way through the guests to where the band were playing. Mapp was the first to make a move and sallied up to Mr. Coward.

'Dear Mr. Coward, so nice to see you again. Elizabeth Mapp-Flint, *chatelaine* of Mallards House.'

Noël held out his hand.

'So pleased you are to meet me, dear lady!'

'How busy you must be Mr. Coward, nodoubt attending countless balls, parties and intimate soirées.'

'Indeed, dear lady.'

'So much Champagne and glittering diamonds,' continued Mapp.

'A diamond is just a piece of charcoal that handled stress exceptionally well, Mrs. Mapp-Flint!' replied Mr. Coward.

'Indeed, dear sir,' agreed Mapp, mistaking the Coward wit for a statement of fact. 'Is that really Trevor Howard and Celia Johnson over there?' continued Mapp.

'Just look-alikes,' joked Noël, 'Hired from a theatrical agency in London, probably.'

Not quite sure whether he was being entirely straight with her, Elizabeth just laughed and made her way back to the Major, who had already consumed several whisky and sodas.

Georgie had been in deep conversation with the current Mayor of Tilling – Albert Clemments who owned a small number of newsagents in the locality. They had been discussing the calls for the ending of food rationing. Mr. Clemments felt particularly sorry for the children who had a very limited supply of chocolate and sweets, which were, of course, available in his outlets.

Lucia managed to catch Georgie's eye and he politely ended the conversation with the Mayor and made his way to her.

'Georgie, I have *ickle* surprise for you,' and she took hold of his hand, guiding him towards the musicians. Seeing Mr. Howard and Miss Johnson, chatting merrily with each other, Georgie was simply lost for words. His heart began to beat faster and he became slightly light-headed.

'Lucia, it isn't is it?'

'It *is*, Georgie! Do come and meet them – they're very nice!'

Georgie shook Trevor Howard's hand – it was reassuringly firm.

'I hear you're a big fan, Sir George,' said Trevor, 'Celia has been looking forward to meeting you.'

'She has?' gasped Georgie.

'Oh, absolutely, Sir George,' replied Miss Johnson. 'I believe you are a great patron of the arts.'

'Well, a patron, certainly, Miss Johnson.'

'Oh, do call me Celia, Sir George.'

'And you must call me Georgie, Celia!'

Noël turned to Johnny Gielgud.

'It's *Brief Encounter* all over again, dear!'

Lucia could not have wished for a better evening. The musicians of the Covent Garden Opera Company – so used to playing Verdi and Wagner for hours on end – delighted with their selection of waltzes, polkas, light classics and arrangements of popular songs. Their rendition of *La Cumparsita* even brought Quaint Irene onto the dance floor, partnered by a very willing Noël Coward. Diva found a suitable partner – a widowed dairy farmer who appeared to own the vast majority of the cows currently grazing in the East Sussex countryside and Evie managed to coax the Padre into performing a slow waltz.

Dinner was nothing less than a triumph and after the last mouthfuls of Lucia's exotic fruit salad had been consumed, Elizabeth David was applauded by all the guests – the loudest applause coming from Lucia herself.

By eleven, cars had begun to arrive to pick up the guests and just before midnight only the Wyses, Bartletts, Quaint Irene (now almost inseparable from Noël Coward), Diva, the Mapp-Flints, Olga and Lucia's celebrity quartet remained. As the musicians packed away their instruments, Lucia suggested a little *po di musica* to round off the evening. Lucia and Georgie played a short extract from the slow movement from Rachmaninov's Second Piano Concerto – now he knew why Lucia had insisted they practise it!

'More drinks anybody?' asked Lucia. 'A little nightcap, perhaps?'
'Perhaps a small glass of water?' replied Noël. 'Just to surprise my liver!'

Gentle laughter showed collective appreciation for yet another example of Mr. Coward's perpetual wit.

'Mr Coward, do you have a little party piece?' enquired Mapp.

'Well…'

'Oh please!' pleaded Mapp, now feeling rather giddy after drinking a little too much Champagne.

'If you insist,' and he sat down at the piano, fingered a few of the keys, needlessly adjusted the music stand and eventually began to sing.

> *I've been to a marvellous party!*
> *At Willows End, Tilling-on-Sea.*
> *Lucia, I'm told*
> *Was so frightfully bold*
> *When constructing the guest list for tea!*
> *The food was divine, my dear lady,*
> *The finest spread I ever saw.*
> *A dance with Miss Coles got me quite in a flap,*
> *She's a dark horse, for sure, but a decent old chap,*
> *And I had hoped Sir George would have sat on my lap!*
> *But I couldn't have liked it more!*

Olga joined him for a final rendition of *Mad Dogs and Englishmen*.

Georgie turned to Miss Johnson.

'I do hope that you have enjoyed your little visit to Tilling.'

'I want to remember every minute, always, always to the end of my days, Georgie,' she replied and gave Georgie a wistful smile.

Soon afterwards, Noël's green Bentley left Willows End. During the course of the evening he had somehow managed to persuade Lucia to provide some financial backing for his next venture, had discussed a possible set design with Irene and, like his hostess, considered the evening to be one of total success.

As the rest of the guests left, Georgie turned to Lucia.
'Thank you for making this such a memorable occasion, Lucia,' and he kissed her gently – not on the cheek but on the lips.
Slightly taken aback, she then smiled warmly.
'*Caro mio, Georgino!*'
Olga looked on, smiling too.

Chapter 20

A few months passed. Willows End became familiar territory for the Pillson's circle of friends, Lucia having hosted several evenings of bridge and the previously abandoned evening of poetry and music. Unfortunately, Debussy failed to make an appearance as Lucia quickly realised that even an almost-approximate rendition of *Prélude à l'après-midi d'un faune* was quite beyond them, despite their best efforts.

'We'll stick to Mozart, Georgie,' she had said. 'I've ordered a *potpourri* of opera themes.'

Mapp continued to host her 'televisual entertainments' – usually midweek as the Roman Ruins tours took up most of her time during the weekend. Whilst numbers were not huge, there was certainly enough interest to make most tours viable with the odd coach party or Boy Scout visit swelling the coffers. By now, the supply of tour guides had virtually run out and the printer had been asked to send another batch.

Grosvenor brought in the post from the box by the main gates. One envelope addressed to Sir George had a handsome engraving of the Royal Opera House on the front. It contained a letter from David Webster indicating that the first stage of the refurbishment of Covent Garden had been completed and that he very much hoped that Sir George and Lady Pillson would be able to attend a Gala Evening of Opera to celebrate this milestone. Miss Olga Bracely would be singing exerpts from *The Magic Flute, Der Rosenkavalier, Carmen* and *Tristan und Isolde,* alongside Gladys Ripley, Richard Lewis and Norman Walker. Karl Rankl would be conducting the orchestra and chorus of the Covent Garden Opera Company. A place in the Royal Box would be reserved for them, of course. Sir George would be invited to unveil a commemorative plaque in the foyer before the Overture.

'The Royal Box, Lucia! Sounds very grand, indeed!'
'And dearest Olga singing,' added Lucia. 'Mozart, Bizet, Wagner and….'
'Strauss, Lucia.'
'Dear Strauss!'
'Richard Strauss, Lucia.'
She faltered for just a second.
'Indeed Georgie. A follower of Nietzsche, I recall. Yes, I remember now, *Der Rosenkavalier* is one of his lighter works.'
Having exhausted her entire knowledge of the composer, she placed the letter on her desk.
'I'll send a reply when I have finished dealing with this week's Trust correspondence, Georgie.'

Lucia had received a steady stream of requests from the residents of Tilling. The move from Mallards to Grebe and then to Willows End had necessitated several notices being printed in the *Hampshire Argus*. Small amounts could be issued very quickly as Lucia had sole discretion. However, larger sums needed to be discussed with

160

Georgie and the Padre. This was slightly awkward as Lucia had eventually turned down the Padre's request for items for the Vicarage (though she had indicated that items for the Church itself would be looked upon much more favourably). In turn (no hint of spite, of course), the Padre had successfully argued against Mr. Wyse's car park request. Quaint Irene, having secured at least ten commissions from Mr. Waldings which were to be sent direct to the States, had withdrawn her request and was considering another property entirely, to be purchased from her own increasing funds. However, Diva's need for larger premises and equipment did seem genuine enough and Lucia had had the pleasurable task of informing her that the Trust would be granting her request in full.

On receiving the notice, Diva had immediately telephoned Willows End to thank Lucia profusely and had then rushed to the High Street with her basket in the hope of being accosted and asked the perennial question 'Any news?' As it was quite late in the day, most marketing had already been completed and only Evie Bartlett could be seen on the High Street, on her way to post a letter.

'Evie! Evie!' called Diva from across the Street.

Evie placed the letter in the post box and gave Diva a little wave. Diva ran across the road, just missing Twemlow's errand boy on his bike.

'You seem a little flustered Diva. Is everything all right?' enquired Evie.

'Just ask me!' continued Diva, now slighty out of breath.

Evie looked rather confused.

'Just ask me!' repeated Diva.

'Ask you what?'

'Ask me if there's any news!'

Diva could be very irritating at times but her heart was in the right place.

'Any news, Diva!'

'Yes. Lots!'

Evie waited for Diva to continue. As a vicar's wife, patience was something that she had in abundance.

'Lucia's come up trumps! Got the money for the extension and oven. Phoned the builder. Got to decide between a Hotpoint or a Belling....' and she carried on, in her telegraphic manner.

Evie listened patiently as Diva outlined her plans for offering cooked lunches twice a week and 'special evenings' – though the exact nature of these remained unclear.

'Must dash, Evie,' and Diva ran off in the direction of the ironmongers, where Algernon Wyse was just leaving.

Georgie had begun painting again and was sat next to his easel in the front gardens of Willows End. Whilst the house was striking (in its way), Georgie was not entirely convinced that it made a suitable subject for his artistic endeavours. Essentially a box, in visual terms it could not compare with a pretty cottage complete with crooked chimney, for example. The views from the garden, however, were quite enchanting, allowing him the opportunity to experiment with several hues of green –

the landscape offering a veritable multitude of possibilities.

Georgie dipped his brush into the water and began to mix chartreuse with viridian. The result pleased his eye and he began to apply a few tentative brush strokes on to the fine Langton paper.

'Parfect!' he exclaimed to himself and added a bolder splash of colour.

'Perhaps if I add a little a little olive or avocado…'

Georgie could hear soft footsteps just behind him.

'Painting or making a salad, Georgie?'

Lucia had left her paperwork for a short period of relaxation in the garden and was now looking over Georgie's shoulder at his fledgling composition.

'Quite delightful, Georgie! Exquisite use of colour!'

'Thank you, Lucia. But I've only used green so far.'

'But how expertly you have used it, Georgie! You've managed to capture the very *essence* of Willows End.'

'Have I really? asked Georgie.

'*Meraviglioso pittura, Gergino mio!*' replied Lucia, 'And remember to sign it *Sir* George, Georgie!'

Foljambe brought out a tray of iced tonic water, with neat slices of lime on a saucer.

'If you don't mind Sir, would it be convenient if I took a few hours off this afternoon? Cadman wants to take me to Folkestone to see his aunt. She's quite ill, Sir.'

'Of course, Foljambe,' replied Georgie.

'And tell Cadman that you can have as much time as you need,' added Lucia.

163

A few minutes later, the Rolls left Willows End.

At dinner that evening, the future of Grebe came under discussion.

'Now that all the repairs have been made, Lucia, are you going to sell Grebe?' asked Georgie.

Lucia was chewing a rather gristly piece of beef. If Georgie had not been staring at her, waiting for a reply, she would have surreptitiously removed it from her mouth and placed it in her napkin, but was forced to swallow the offending morsel instead.

'I have given that a lot of thought, Georgie. I'm sure that, if placed on the market, Grebe would sell – it's in a far better condition now than ever before.'

'No thanks to Mapp though!' exclaimed Georgie. 'She let the whole place fall apart around her. And that hole in the ceiling!'

'Poor Elizabeth!' giggled Lucia. 'Imagine her little legs dangling in mid-air! Those poor fireman – what a sight they must have seen!'

'We shouldn't laugh, Lucia. Really we shouldn't.' But Georgie had a big grin on his face.

'Anyway, what about Grebe?' he continued.

Lucia paused – a pause of such length that Georgie knew that she was about to say something of significance.

'I have decided to gift Grebe to the National Trust, Georgie. They already own Blakeney Point in Norfolk and the salt marshes here are of equal national importance.'

'Well that seems like a capital idea, Lucia.'

'And, Georgie, I have also someone in mind to be the custodian of Grebe, though I need to discuss this with the Trustees first.'

'Do tell, Lucia.'

'Our dear Irene Coles, Georgie. You remember how often she used to visit Grebe when I first moved to Tilling? She would sit at the window, looking out over the salt marshes, positively drinking in the atmosphere and make little sketches in her notepad.'

'Yes, I remember, Lucia. You were her Angel and Grebe was her Heaven.'

'The sea is one of art's greatest inspirations, Georgie,' continued Lucia. 'She was so disappointed when Elizabeth moved there.'

Georgie continued to listen as Lucia outlayed her plans in full.

Chapter 21

This opera house has been extensively modernised and extended thanks to the generous patronage of Sir George Pillson, Bart. and Lady Pillson

There was a cheery round of applause as Georgie unveiled the plaque in the foyer of the Royal Opera House, David Webster stood by his side. Georgie had originally contemplated leaving the wording of the plaque as he had originally seen it in Webster's office, with no mention of Lucia and then briefly entertained adding her name but in much smaller letters – Aureus-like. However, he was quite content for the plaque to mention them both in equal terms – after all, it was Lucia's fortune that had been raided!

'Now for the show, Sir George, Lady Pillson', said Mr. Webster. 'I'll join you as soon as I can. Charlie will show you to the Royal Box,' and a young man, impeccably dressed in a smart burgundy uniform – presumably Charlie – took them upstairs, along a long, narrow corridor and through a rather nondescript set of double doors into the Royal Box, which was, to Georgie's disappointment, completely empty.

'The Royal guests will be arriving shortly, Sir,' said Charlie, as he showed Georgie and Lucia to their seats. 'The King, perhaps?' enquired Georgie.

Charlie shrugged his shoulders.

'I'll be along with some Champagne soon, Sir.'

'I doubt that the King will be coming, Georgie,' said Lucia. 'He has been quite ill recently and cannot undertake public engagements for at least three weeks.'

'Was that in the papers? asked Georgie, innocently. 'The last thing I read was that the King's health was improving.'

Lucia stumbled. She had been meaning to tell Georgie about her growing friendship with Princess Elizabeth for months, but the longer she left it the more difficult this seemed. What exactly should she tell him? Certainly not everything! She had shared conversations with the Princess that were highly sensitive and personal – never to be disclosed to anyone. Only last week she had had a long telephone conversation with the Princess whilst Georgie was visiting the High Street, when she had learnt of the King's current health.

'Georgie,' whispered Lucia. 'I've got something to tell you. It's about…'

At that moment the double doors opened and Princess Elizabeth accompanied by her husband, Prince Philip, the Duke of Edinburgh appeared. Georgie bowed and Lucia curtseyed.

'No need for formalities, Lucia. You have met Philip before, haven't you?'

Georgie, wide-eye and speechless, looked at Lucia.

'Yes, at Sandringham. We played croquet, I believe.'

'Croquet, Lucia?' gasped Georgie. 'At Sandringham?'

167

'Pleased to meet you Pillson,' and the Duke held out his hand. 'Hear we've got *you* to thank for all this.'

'Well...'

'Look!' interrupted Lucia, 'Maestro Rankl is about to conduct the orchestra,' and all four took their seats, Lucia and the Princess in the middle, with the Prince and George at either side.

Georgie hardly heard the opening Overture – a thrilling performance of *Die Fledermaus* by the other Strauss – as numerous questions swirled around in his mind. It was quite obvious that Lucia had been hiding something from him – something rather important it seemed. But he would have to wait a little before he heard the full story.

As the orchestra's closing chords were played, Charlie appeared with the Champagne and a small bottle of whisky for the Duke.

'Fill her up, son,' said Prince Philip. 'I'm going to be stuck here for at least three hours! Last time I was here they were performing Wagner. That's the kind of opera that starts at six o' clock and after its been droning on for three hours, it's still only six thirty!'

'Really, Philip!' said the Princess, 'Lucia and Sir George are opera lovers and Miss Bracely is a personal friend of theirs.'

'A bit of a looker, eh Pillson? Great pair of lungs, I'd say.'

Georgie felt himself nod politely, whilst turning a shade of crimson.

'Dear Olga's coming on stage now, Georgie.'

Lucia looked at her programme – *The Queen of the Night Aria* from *The Magic Flute* was one of their favourites.

As the applause died down, the doors opened again and David Webster, accompanied by James Chuter Ede, the Home Secretary, made their way into the Royal Box. Introductions were brief as the next piece of music was about to begin as Olga was joined on stage by the tenor, Richard Lewis. They made a perfect Tamino and Pamina, thought Lucia.

'The Home Secretary wants a private word, Sir George, in the interval,' whispered Mr. Webster.

Again, Georgie was distracted from the music as he began to think of possible reasons why the Home Secretary might want a word with him. His head began to spin slightly as the terrible thought entered his mind that the Aureus deception had been discovered. Perhaps the Home Secretary was about to rescind his knighthood? He touched his Insignia, just to check that it was still there, pinned to his jacket.

After what seemed like an age, Georgie stood to stretch his legs as the interval began.

'Better go to my office, Sir George,' said David Webster, ominously, 'It's a little more private in there.'

In the office, Mr. Chuter Ede was already sat at David Webster's desk, looking through several papers. Georgie approached the Home Secretary, feeling rather like a naughty schoolboy about to be chastised by the headmaster.

'Sit down, Pillson. Webster, no need for you to stay.'

Georgie gulped. Mr. Chuter Ede was known as a no-nonsense politician, used to getting his way.

'We've been keeping an eye on you Pillson,' continued the Home Secretary.

'Really?' responded Georgie, weakly.

'Recently knighted, I see,' he added as he scanned through the information infront of him.

'For services to the arts. I helped fund the renovations here.'

'Yes, Pillson, I know all about that. And the Aureus too.'

Georgie gulped again. Beads of sweat began to appear on his brow.

'Is there a problem, Home Secretary?'

'Not at all Pillson. We're just looking for a few chaps of the right calibre to join the Festival of Britain Executive Committee – new blood and all that. The Prime Minister mentioned your name.'

Georgie managed to stifle a huge sigh of relief.

'Well that would be quite an honour, Home Secretary.'

'It would mean spending a couple of days a week, here in London, Pillson. I take it that Lady Pillson would not object?'

'I'm sure Lady Pillson will be quite accommodating, Home Secretary.'

'Next meeting at Number 10, a week on Tuesday. Check the details with Barbara, my secretary,' and he gave Georgie a card.

'Must dash, Pillson. Opera not really my thing!'

A beaming Georgie returned to the Royal Box.

'I take it that the Home Secretary had some good news for you, Sir George?' asked David Webster.

The conversations stopped and all eyes were on Georgie.

'Well, as a leading benefactor to the nation, I've been asked to join the Festival of Britain Executive Committee and I have, of course, agreed!'

'Congratulations, Sir George!' said Princess Elizabeth. 'The King has taken a keen personal interest in the project and Philip's seen the plans for the Skylon.'

'Great British engineering, Pillson! Have they asked you to pay for it yet?' joked the Duke.

'I'm sure that Sir George will be able to apply his talents to any task set before him,' replied Lucia and passed him a glass of Champagne.

Georgie could now relax and enjoy the rest of the Gala Evening - extracts from *Der Rosenkavalier* and *Carmen* and an impromptu performance specially for Georgie of *For He's a Jolly Good Fellow* sung by Olga accompanied by the massed chorus of the Covent Garden Opera Company.

The Princess and Duke left immediately afterwards and David Webster invited Lucia and Georgie to tour backstage.

'We've been able to make some improvements to the dressing rooms, much to the delight of the chorus and orchestra and the lighting rig has been extensively modernised.'

Lucia nodded, feigning a degree of interest, though, in truth, talk of dressing rooms and rigs failed to excite her, even just a little.

'Let's see if Miss Bracely is ready,' and Mr. Webster knocked on the door of Dressing Room Number One.

'Enter!' bellowed Olga.

Olga looked even more larger than life than usual as she had still to remove the copious amounts of stage make-up, without which even those with the ruddiest of complexions would appear pale and gaunt on stage.

'*Bel canto*, Olga!' enthused Lucia.

'It was just wonderful, Olga,' added Georgie, a hint of a tear in his eye and they embraced.

'How about a spot of dinner?' asked David Webster. 'I've booked a table at the Waldorf Hotel. Gladys, Richard and Norman have been invited too. No expenses spared!'

'Sounds like my kind of dinner!' said Olga. 'I wonder whether they will have any oysters left….?'

Chapter 22

Breaking the habit of not buying a daily newspaper, Major Mapp-Flint walked back to Mallards with the *The Times* under his arm, having been alerted to its contents a few minutes earlier by Algernon Wyse. The Major had listened patiently to Mr. Wyses' enthusiastic description of an article on page four of the publication but doubted whether Elizabeth would share his delight.

Elizabeth had a slight cold and was feeling rather under the weather, the dose of Beecham's Powders she had taken earlier that morning had yet to have an effect.

'Better look at this, Liz-girl,' said the Major, handing Mapp the newspaper. 'Page four.'

Mapp turned over the pages to reveal a large photograph showing Lucia, Georgie, Princess Elizabeth and the Duke of Edinburgh standing in the Royal Box, Covent Garden. Mapp read out loud the accompanying article.

'Generous benefactors Sir George and Lady Pillson were joined by Princess Elizabeth and the Duke of Edinburgh for last night's Gala Evening of Opera to celebrate the renovation of the Royal Opera House. Those performing alongside the orchestra and chorus of the Covent Garden Opera Company conducted by Karl Rankl included Olga Bracely…..'

Mapp stopped reading and threw the paper aside. It was the photograph that particularly irked her. There Lucia was, stood next to the future Queen, smiles on both their faces, for the whole world to see.

'Must have donated a tidy sum,' ventured the Major, curious to know the precise figures involved.

'We'll never hear the end of it, Benjy. Princess Elizabeth this, Princess Elizabeth that! It wouldn't surprise me if Lucia starts to tell all and sundry they're now the best of friends!'

'Steady on, old girl! They probably hardly spoke a word to each other.'

'Whatever, Benjy. That won't stop Lucia bragging and spinning her tales.'

She scrutinised the photograph once more, reached for her handkerchief and blew for England.

Georgie sat eating his first boiled egg, his second being kept warm by one of his newly-crocheted egg cosies. It was quite late in the morning but as they had arrived back from London in the early hours, he had stayed in bed, unlike Lucia who had risen at her normal hour. After arriving back at Willows End, Lucia had told Georgie about meeting the Princess at the Investiture – though none of the finer details – and how she had been invited to Sandringham. A Royal whim, nodoubt! She explained that she'd not told Georgie about this as it had been the weekend when he had arranged to meet Olga in Liverpool and she knew that he was so looking forward to it. She had also met the Princess at Norman Hartnell's studios and had a few brief telephone conversations on very trivial matters. Georgie seemed quite happy with her explanations, which had been carefully formulated on the drive back to Tilling. Feeling slightly guilty for not sharing absolutely everything with her husband, she readily agreed that spending two consecutive days a week in London was entirely appropriate for Georgie's new role on the Festival of Britain Executive Committee.

Lucia entered the room. She had been out in the garden planting a trug full of daffodil and crocus bulbs and had sketched in her notebook a possible design for a vegetable patch.

'Carrots and potatoes, Georgie, peas and marrows. Perhaps some runner beans,' and she showed Georgie her drawings.

'And perhaps I could start a herb garden, Lucia?' replied Georgie.

'Such a good idea, Georgie. I have given cook lots of Elizabeth's recipes which do require an extensive herbal repertoire.' She paused. 'Elizabeth *David*, Georgie.'

'I know that Lucia! Mapp probably suffered from herbal ignorance before she stole your recipe for *Lobster à la Riseholme*!'

Lucia didn't respond. Although it had happened so many tears ago, the thought of Mapp rummaging through her kitchen cupboards and drawers at Grebe in order to find her secret recipe still sent a small shiver down her spine.

'And we must discuss London, Lucia,' continued Georgie. 'I will need to arrange overnight accommodation once a week for the next few months. Olga mentioned at dinner last night that the Ritz is just a ten minute walk from Downing Street. That would be most convenient.'

She had also mentioned (after consuming a large plate of oysters and several glasses of Champagne) that if he promised not to snore he could sleep on the sofa in her lounge. However, Georgie decided not to mention this to Lucia. He also resolved not to mention it to Olga too – chances were that she would have no recollection of their whispered conversation, anyhow.

'Dear Olga – always so helpful! Then the Ritz it must be, Georgie!'

'Capital, Lucia!' and he began his second boiled egg.

News of Lucia and Georgie's evening with the Princess and Duke was the most discussed topic of the day on Tilling High Street as the question 'Any News?' was both eagerly awaited and answered. Mr. Wyse had obviously told his wife immediately after returning to Starling Cottage, Susan had told Diva, who had spoken to Evie, who had bumped into Quaint Irene and soon the whole crowd were sat in Diva's tea-shop sipping cups of tea and eating jam puffs – a large bowl of them placed on the centre of the table. Janet was still struggling with the larger capacity of the new oven and baking rather too many cakes and pastries and given that recent visitors to the Roman Ruins had continued their steady decline in numbers, there was a glut of jam puffs at the moment.

Just as Diva was about to replenish the bowl, Elizabeth and the Major appeared.

'Seen the paper, Elizabeth?' asked Diva.

All eyes were on Mapp as they awaited her response. When it came, it was not the one they had expected.

'So gratifying to see our dear Lulu amongst the *bosom* of our Royalty. As Tillingites, we should be very proud of our former Worship.'

There was an awkward silence which Diva was the first to break.

'I wonder if she invited them to Willows End? There might be another party!'

'I very much doubt that, Godiva dear. The Princess and Duke see literally hundreds of people every week at all kinds of events. I dare say they exchanged the odd word or too….'

'A photograph doesn't lie, Mapp,' interrupted Irene. 'You can see it in their expressions.'

'What on earth are you talking about, Quaint one?' said Mapp.

'There's a look of familiarity between them – an artist can detect the signs, Mapp. My Angel and the Princess!'

'Oh, what nonsense, Irene!'

'Of course, it is entirely possible that they have met before,' added Mr. Wyse. 'Most likely at Sir George's Investiture.'

'Along with *thousands* of others,' continued Mapp, spitting out the number.

Chapter 23

Georgie quickly settled into a routine as he visited London by train every Wednesday and Thurday, staying at the Ritz overnight. Occasionally he had very little to do and would spend the best part of the day visiting the Festival site itself, marvelling at the speed of the building works that were transforming the area and became a familiar figure to the workmen. He wore a small enamelled Festival badge on his lapel which gave him access to all areas. Mostly, however, he was involved in seemingly interminable finance meetings where officials in suits read out long lists of figures to collectively raised eyebrows.

Right from the start it had been explained to Georgie that his valuable work as a committee member was, of course, unpaid. Lucia was both surprised and a little annoyed to learn that there would also be no expenses paid and that it would be she footing the entire bill for her husband's period of public office.

'On no accounts agree to giving any money without my consent first,' she had said. However, just a few weeks after those words were uttered, Georgie realised some misunderstanding must have occurred when the minutes of a previous meeting were being read out stating that 'Sir George Pillson agreed to make a donation to the Skylon project.'

'Did I really?' whispered Georgie to the man in the grey suit sitting next to him.

'Five thousand, I believe,' came the reply.
'Gosh!' exclaimed Georgie, out loud.

Lucia would spend the days when Georgie was away on Trust matters. There seemed no end of need in Tilling, despite the promises of the Labour government. Some of the letters and requests she received (almost) moved her to tears. Although she had never experienced anything remotely like poverty herself, she was beginning to appreciate the desperation a lack of money can cause. Passing on a few pounds to those who genuinely needed help lifted her soul.

Amongst other things, the Lady Pillson Charitable Trust had provided a new twenty-four volume revised fourteenth edition of the *Encyclopedia Britannica* for Tilling Library and new crockery, cutlery and a Baby Burco for the Church Hall. Presently, an application to commission a statue of local playwright John Fletcher who, allegedly, had supplied Shakespeare with some of his best lines was being considered. Lucia relished the delightful prospect of an official unveiling ceremony with accompanying *tableaux vivants* where she might reprise her role as Good Queen Bess.

Throughout this period, Lucia remained in contact with Princess Elizabeth. She visited Buckingham Palace once ('so nice to be back!') and Kensington Palace where the Princess introduced her to Princess Alice, a lady of similar age to Lucia herself. Lucia spent a very pleasant hour drinking strong black coffee and learning the reasons behind Princess Alice's strong aversion to both tea and milk.

Within Tilling itself, life carried on as normal with just the odd variation to stifle monotony. Diva's tea-shop had been extended and now seemed emptier than ever mid-week. However, come the weekend and a modicum of sunshine, the extra tables and chairs were put to good use and Janet could put the new oven through its paces. Quaint Irene was busy with her commissions and experimenting with the latest acrylic paints. She had jumped at Lucia's offer of becoming custodian of Grebe and was now in the process of packing her belongings, ready for the move, the date of which would be ultimately decided by the National Trust. The Wyses had decided to buy their own television set and given the march of technology, had purchased one with a larger screen, sharper picture and superior sound to the model incumbent in the Mapp-Flint household, for twenty guineas less. As a result of this purchase, they politely declined any further invitations to Mapp's televisual entertainments. Neither did they advertise any of their own. Evie Bartlett had begun reading Trollope's *Chronicles of Barsetshire* where clerical dealings of a fictional nature seemed so much more engaging than those in real life. Kenneth professed that he didn't read fiction at all, though Evie secretly wondered how much of the Good Book might be classed as such.

Chapter 24

'In this Festival, we look back with pride and forward with resolution.'

King George stood on the steps of St. Paul's Cathedral and declared the Festival of Britain open. Behind him, amongst the throng of dignitaries, stood Sir George and Lady Pillson, distinguished guests of His Majesty's Government. Later on they planned to attend a special service of dedication at the Royal Festival Hall and visit the Dome of Discovery, the Telekinema and the new wing of the Science Museum.

As they walked through the Festival Pleasure Gardens, Lucia looked up at the Skylon, towering three hundred feet in the air.

'And how much of that did I pay for, Georgie?' she asked.

'About the last ten foot, I should think!' replied Georgie.

'Is that all?' said Lucia, shaking her head.

'It *was* rather expensive, Lucia. But isn't it magnificent?'

Of all the Festival buildings and exhibitions, it was the Skylon that Georgie held dear to his heart. Seemingly floating in the air with no visible means of support (just like the British economy joked its detractors), it was a feat of engineering brilliance. Georgie had lunched with its designers, Philip Powell and Hidalgo Moya, and had told them all about *his* inspiration for Willows End.

'We must organise a coach party to visit here, Georgie. The Wyses, the Padre and Evie, dear Diva and Irene…'

'And the Mapp-Flints, Lucia?'

'Of course, Georgie!' replied Lucia, dismissing from her mind memories of the Tenterden fête coach incident. 'We'll have luncheon at the Riverside Restaurant. I'm sure that Irene will appreciate the Ben Nicholson mural.'

'And Mapp will certainly appreciate the cream cakes!' quipped Georgie.

'There's the Archbishop of Cantebury, Benjy,' said Mapp, pointing to the little screen of her television set.

'The one with the funny hat?' replied the Major.

The Mapp-Flints were watching the BBC coverage of the opening ceremony of the Royal Festival Hall. Unusally, Withers had been allowed to join them in their viewing.

'I haven't seen Lady Pillson yet, ma'am,' said Withers. 'Or Sir George.'

'I very much doubt they have a front row seat, Withers,' replied Mapp who was very much hoping that their presence on the South Bank would remain undocumented. 'Probably sat in the Gods,' she added.

'That sounds rather grand, ma'am,' continued Withers.

'Not at all, Withers!' chuckled Mapp. 'It's like being at the back of the queue.'

'Well at least they're in the queue, ma'am,' replied Withers, not so innocently.

Mapp gave Withers a piercing look.

'More tea, I think, Withers. And cut *two* slices of chocolate cake, will you?'

Mapp presumed that the Wyses were also watching the broadcast at Starling Cottage. Susan had intimated earlier that week that she would be wearing her MBE all day as a way of joining in with the national celebrations. Diva had strung Union Jack bunting around her tea-shop and was offering 'the best of British fare' consisting primarily of corned beef sandwiches – the Brazilian origins of which had been rather overlooked, though this did not seem to bother the Padre and Evie, who polished off a whole plateful. Several thousand miles away, Quaint Irene and Lucy were feasting on steak, fries and apple pie, courtesy of Irvine B. Waldings.

That evening Lucia and Georgie attended a concert of British music at the Royal Festival Hall, jointly conducted by Maestros Sargent and Boult (in turn, rather than together, as Lucia later explained to Diva). Olga, who had been due to sing *Rule Britannia* at the end of the concert had had to be replaced at the last minute due to her almost choking on a Vocalzone Throat Pastille – a misadventure that Georgie was later to find out was not uncommon amongst professional singers. She remained backstage, drinking copious amounts of water as her replacement sang Thomson's immortal lines.

Georgie nudged Lucia with his elbow in order to gain her attention.
'What's happened to Olga?' he whispered.
'Shush, Georgie!'
'She's supposed to be singing *Rule Britannia*!'
'Shush!' repeated Lucia, a little louder this time.

183

Georgie emitted an uncharacteristic large sigh and checked his wristwatch. The concert was due to finish in just a few minutes. He would rush backstage and find out what had happened.

As the conductors left the platform for the final time and the applause began to dwindle, Georgie and Lucia (rather reluctantly) left their seats and made their way to the backstage doors.

'I'm looking for Miss Olga Bracely,' said Georgie as a pair of bassoonists passed by.

'Miss Bracely, the singer?' asked one.

'Yes,' replied Georgie. 'She was meant to be singing *Rule Britannia*.'

'Choked on a Vocalzone, I heard,' replied the other.

Georgie gave Lucia a look of panic.

'But she's fine now,' continued the first bassoonist. 'She was chatting to the Principal Clarinet just two minutes ago.'

'Thank goodness for that!' Georgie looked visibly relieved.

'And what lovely playing tonight, gentlemen,' added Lucia. 'Bassoons – such, such….. distinguished instruments.' She had wanted to use the word 'comical' but did not want to offend the helpful gentlemen.

It did not take long to find Olga. She could be heard quite clearly amongst the hubbub backstage as she sang the last verse of the Arne *a cappella* to an appreciative audience of viola players in one of the dressing rooms.

'Georgie!' shrieked Olga as she caught sight of Georgie and Lucia and rushed to embrace him.

'You'll never guess what happened, Georgie,' and she coughed loudly and began clearing her throat – a dramatic gesture rather than a necessity, perhaps.

'Two bassoonists just told us. What a dreadful shame. I was so looking forward to you singing.'

'Sorry to disappoint, Georgie. *Oo vewy cwoss?*'

Lucia gave Olga a stern look. It was she who spoke baby talk to Georgie, not Olga.

Georgie shook his head and laughed.

'Dear Olga. How could I ever be cross with you? Do join us for something to eat at our hotel. I'm famished and I expect you are too!'

As they ate their meal in the Winter Garden Restaurant at the Strand Palace Hotel, Lucia could not help thinking about Georgie and Olga. From the very moment she had moved to Riseholme, all those years ago, it was clear that they held each other in great affection. That had never concerned Lucia, or indeed Olga's husband, the late Mr. Shuttleworth. However, as the years passed, there were certain times when this affection seemed to border on something altogether stronger and although she would not admit it to herself, Lucia occasionally felt the pangs of jealousy. When Olga was around, Georgie's eyes sparkled. He didn't spend hours sitting with needle and thread or express any desire to polish his bibelots. In Olga's company he was always laughing and smiling and nothing was too tar'some.

Despite the rigours of the day, Lucia had no real appetite and picked at her food. Eventually she laid down her knife and fork.

'Please forgive me, Georgie, but I seem to have developed a headache. Such a busy day. I think I will retire early. Goodnight Georgie. Goodnight, Olga.'

'Don't worry Lucia,' replied Olga. 'I'll look after him!' and gave Georgie's arm a little squeeze.

'Goodnight Lucia,' said Georgie as Lucia made her way to the lobby.

'Let's choose a dessert, Georgie!'

'I know it's rather late, Georgie, but one of the trombone players told me that there's a lock-in at the Lamb and Flag tonight. The whole brass section will be there, some fiddlers and half the woodwind players.'

'A lock-in?' repeated Georgie, giving Olga a quizzical look.

'Oh, Georgie!' Olga bellowed. 'Such an innocent! Let's get a cab.'

'But what about Lucia?' asked a concerned Georgie.

'She'll be fast asleep by now. Come on, let's have a little fun,' and she called the maître d'hôtel over to order a taxi.

'Another brandy, Georgie?' asked Olga, words slightly slurred, her own glass now empty again.

They had been at the Lamb and Flag for well over an hour and many of the musicians were starting to leave, instruments in tow. The two bassoonists Georgie had met earlier that day were sat on the next table.

'How do you get two bassoonists to play in tune?' bellowed Olga in their direction. The two men, now rather the worse for wear themselves, shrugged their shoulders.

'Shoot one of them!' came the answer and Olga roared with laughter, slamming the table with her hand.

'Come on Georgie. It's getting late. Time for bed!' and she grabbed his arm.

It was Georgie who first saw the flashing blue light of the police car that had just pulled up beside the pub front door. Two officers got out of the vehicle and began to knock insistently. The publican – a jolly decent chap thought Georgie – had no option but to open up and let the officers in, as glasses of all shapes and sizes, both full and empty, were quickly hidden behind the bar.

The taller of the two policemen surveyed the scene – a familiar sight – as the publican tried his best to explain that this was indeed a private function following the concert at the Royal Festival Hall. A group of string players were nervously clutching their violin cases, looking not dissimilar to the American gangsters depicted by Hollywood. The policeman appeared to be listening sympathetically to the publican and after a short discussion with his colleague he spoke to the crowd.

'You've all had your fun and we haven't room at the Police Station for the lot of you, so clear off back home! And no trouble on the way back!'

There was a grateful murmur of approval, and the revellers began to leave.

Olga approached the officer. Alcohol had given her an additional level of confidence that is not always beneficial in these situations.

'I object to you telling me to 'clear off', young man. And so does my friend.'

Georgie looked aghast at Olga. Sometimes it was better to just keep quiet.

'Really, madam?' replied the officer. 'And you are…?'

'Miss Olga Bracely, the famous soprano,' chipped in Georgie.

'Never heard of her!' replied the policeman. 'Have you Bert?'

The second policeman shook his head.

'And this is Sir George Pillson, young man. SIR George, Realm of the Knight!' Olga hiccupped loudly.

The two policeman gave each other a meaningful look. They had spotted Georgie's Insignia, which was now perilously close to falling off his lapel.

'Sir George, is it?' asked the second officer.

Georgie was beginning to feel flustered and a little faint.

'Yes, Officer. I do apologise for Miss Bracely's tone of voice – perhaps a little too much Champagne!'

'Well, we could always take Miss Bracely to the Station, if necessary.'

'Perhaps I could just call a cab for us both?' asked Georgie.

'No, I think it would be better for you both to step into the police car, Sir.'

Any remaining colour immediately drained from Georgie's face as he contemplated a night spent at the Police Station, a story in the press and, worst of all, a humiliating confrontation with Lucia. To cap it all, Olga began to make strange growling sounds, the like of which Georgie had never heard Olga emit before.

'And we'll drop you off at your hotel, Sir. The night's still young!' and the policeman winked at Georgie.

'Miss Bracely has separate accommodation, Officer,' replied a rather embarrassed Georgie.

Dressing for bed in the dark, for he did not wish to disturb Lucia, Georgie felt a great sense of relief that the British class system was still very much alive despite two world wars and several Labour governments. A title gave one a huge degree of priviledge and respect and could, thankfully, get one out of the odd scrape or two.

Lucia, who had been unable to settle ever since she had returned to the room, glanced at the luminescent face of the bedside clock. It was two in the morning. Where on earth had Georgie been?

Chapter 25

'This is London. It is with the greatest sorrow that we make the following announcement: It was announced from Sandringham at 10.45 today, February 6th 1952, that the King who retired to rest last night in his usual health, passed peacefully away in his sleep earlier this morning.'
BBC Home Service.

Although the sad news was not a great shock, given the King's long period of illness and recent operation, as with any death, there was a profound feeling of loss and despair which was felt throughout the whole country and beyond.

The normally busy streets of Tilling were deserted, most of the shop-keepers having closed early on hearing the news, and the Union Jack flew at half mast atop Tilling Town Hall. Outside the Church, the Padre had erected a large sign notifying his parishioners of a special service of remembrance to be held that evening.

Georgie sat listening to the radio, where snippets of information about the King were given inbetween suitably sombre music. Although Georgie had only spoken briefly to His Majesty at his Investiture and at the Festival of Britain Opening Ceremony, he was quite numbed by the news. On hearing the announcement, Lucia had shed a brief tear and had written a very short note of condolence to the new Queen who would be arriving back in Britain from Kenya shortly. On the back of the envelope she wrote the secret code word in the top left hand corner, ensuring that her missive would be passed both immediately and directly to the Queen.

That evening, Tilling Church was as full as the Padre had expected and the congregation were packed into every available space. Never had the choir stalls been so full. The service was simple but poignant as the the Padre paid tribute to a man who had endeared himself to the Nation, not just as a result of his wartime leadership, but equally his dedication to his subjects and loyal sense of duty. The Padre reminded everyone that, as with any period of darkness, light would emerge triumphant and the Padre spoke of the dawn of a new Elizabethan age.

The service ended with the National Anthem – the Padre helpfully reminding the congregation that they were singing 'God save the Queen.' It seemed rather odd singing the new words. Lucia was momentarily transported back over fifty years, singing in praise of an elderly Queen Victoria.

Elizabeth was formally declared Queen on February 8th at St. James' Palace.

The King's funeral procession was broadcast on the television on 15th February. Mapp and the Major watched the proceedings alone. It didn't seem the right thing to invite guests.

Chapter 26

As the months passed, the collective grief of the Nation began to dissipate and a new feeling of optimism began to emerge. There was even talk of rationing being ended. The new Queen, with Churchill as her guide, seemed to demonstrate an extraordinary level of wisdom for someone so young. This was, of course, no surprise to Lucia.

In Tilling, the High Street was busy, the daily question of 'Any news?' eliciting a variety of animated responses – the raising of eyebrows, the pursing of lips or the shrugging of shoulders to name but three. In tribute to the new Queen, Diva's tea-shop now served Queen of Puddings and Mr. Wyse had taken to wearing a red rose in his lapel. Quaint Irene was in the process of painting a large Elizabethan mural on the wall of the dining room at Grebe – without the approval of the National Trust. Lucia had seen her rough sketch and her nod was the only approval Irene felt was necessary.

Georgie sat in his Bibelot Room (a brass plaque now giving it 'official' status) where his precious objects were housed in three bespoke mahogany cabinets. These were glass fronted and the mirrored backs reflected the brilliance of some of the trinkets that were on display. Of course, Georgie never thought of his collection as a random assortment of trinkets. In fact, he abhorred the word and refused to accept the Chambers definition, common to many dictionaries, that a bibelot was *indeed* a trinket.

His collection had suffered somewhat at the hands of the light-fingered Guru many years ago, but with the subsequent years, had now grown to impressive proportions, from his Queen Anne silver toy porringer which he had received as a boy to a newly-acquired gold-set cameo, featuring bathing muses. The subject was not particularly to his taste but the craftwork involved in producing the said object was simply stunning. Other interesting items included a small ivory carving of a man with a rather large beard, bequeathed to him by Poppy, Duchess of Sheffield, a rather handsome gold matchbox case engraved with birds in flight and signed in Cyrillic script and a small green-enameled box, supposedly holding a lock of Lord Byron's hair.

There was a gentle tap on the door. Foljambe entered.
'Yes, Foljambe?' enquired Georgie.
'Begging your pardon, Sir, but I have a delicate matter to discuss with you.'
Georgie's ears pricked up.
'It's Cadman's aunt, Sir,' continued Foljambe.
'Yes, I was sorry to hear the sad news. I hope the funeral went well…. as well as can be expected, of course.'
'Thank you, Sir. Just to inform you Sir, she's left us her house – on the seafront, Sir.'
Georgie didn't respond. He was waiting for the next sentence.

'It's quite a large house, Sir and we were thinking, Cadman and I, that we might start up our own Bed and Breakfast business. It seems an opportunity too good to miss, Sir. And we're both not getting any younger.'

Georgie remained quiet.

'Well, actually Sir, we *have* decided to move to Folkestone… and…'

'And has Cadman spoken to Lady Pillson on this matter?' interupted Georgie, rather tersely.

'Oh yes Sir. This morning. She has already accepted his resignation and wished us 'good luck' for the future.'

'Has she indeed!' replied Georgie, somewhat uncharitably.

'You can come a stay at any time, Sir. Lady Pillson too. We hope to open up in time for the late summer season. There'll be a lovely double room, Sir. Or perhaps two singles?'

Georgie had wanted to plead with Foljambe to stay. It had worked before and surely she and Cadman were pleased with their handsome accommodation above the garage and workshop? Couldn't they just sell the house, which would provide a little nest egg for their retirement? However, on reflection, Foljambe had given Georgie so many years' unstinting service that it seemed selfish in the extreme to persuade her to change her plans and dash her dreams. Therefore, with a heavy heart, Georgie gave her his blessing just a few minutes later.

'It's too tar'some, Lucia!' exclaimed Georgie as he entered the garden-room.

'She's told you then?' replied Lucia, sat at her desk.

'And I'm not even particularly keen on Folkestone! Too many buckets and spades!'

'I tend to agree, Georgie, but it does have a few merits.'

'Such as?'

Lucia thought for a while and decided to move the conversation on.

'I have in mind the perfect replacements, Georgie.'

'But how can I ever replace Foljambe, Lucia?'

'Georgino mio! No-one is irreplaceable. Not even Foljambe! And remember Georgie that *I* am losing Cadman.'

'Well it's not quite the same is it?' He paused. 'Who do you suggest then?'

When Lucia told Georgie, he raised his eyebrows but seemed to acquiesce.

'Then that's agreed, Georgie. I'll write to them straight away then arrange a meeting, if they are agreeable.'

'Leaving next week, Benjy!'

Withers had told Mapp about Cadman and Foljambe just a few minutes after hearing the news from Grosvenor on the High Street. She had been told – in confidence – by Foljambe herself. Grosvenor was not usually one to break a confidence, but in this instance, the news seemed so momentous that, despite her best efforts, she could not keep it contained.

'Wonder how Pillson will cope,' replied the Major, 'Without his nursemaid!'

Mapp gave Benjy a stern look but said nothing to contradict him.

'It will certainly be hard to replace Foljambe, Benjy. I can't imagine how *we* would ever cope without Withers.'

'Rather well,' thought the Major – a young, fresh-faced maid around the house would be rather invigorating.

'And Cadman will be sorely missed too,' added Mapp, thinking more of her own situation as Cadman's duties regularly involved picking up those lacking transport of their own – such as the Mapp-Flints – and driving them to and from Willows End, which was a fair walk from the main town.

'Good chap that Cadman,' said the Major. 'A man's man! Not so many of them in Tilling!'

On the contrary, thought Elizabeth.

After finishing the letter offering the positions soon to be available at Willows End, Lucia turned her attention to another letter – to the new Minister for Transport, Alan Lennox-Boyd. For many years Lucia had toyed with the idea of establishing the Royal Fish Express as a means of reviving the Tilling fishing industry. In medieval times, Tilling fish had been transported to the Royal table by pack-horses and mules. Today the railways offered a much quicker and infinitely more hygienic method of delivery. She had been previously rebuffed when putting forward the idea to the relevant authorities but now, with a Coronation being planned, it seemed an ideal time to try once more. Georgie had established some connections in Whitehall and Lucia knew that the Queen had once considered becoming a pescatarian, following a banquet on foreign soil where she had politely chewed her way through a chunk of raw caribou.

'Alan Lennox-Boyd, Georgie. Have you met him?'

Georgie, more half-asleep than half-awake as he lazed upon the sofa, the May sunshine filtering through into the garden-room, took a minute to recall the name.

'The railways man? Nice chap. Met him a couple of times in London at some planning meetings for the Festival.'

'Well, I want you to have a word with him about this,' and she thrust the letter she had just written under his nose for perusal.

'Not that old chestnut again, Lucia!' sighed Georgie. 'It's so old hat!'

'Georgie! Now is the *ideal* time to revive the idea. Her Majesty is very partial to *les fruits de mer*.'

'Just as I am, Lucia, but I am perfectly capable of visiting the local fishmonger on the High Street to satisfy my craving for scallops and crayfish. I'm sure that Billingsgate Market is able to supply all the fish the Palace requires.'

'That is not the point Georgie! We have to do our best to uphold our English traditions. The Virgin Queen feasted on Tilling turbot, I believe,' replied Lucia. 'And, with the greatest of repect, Georgie, you are not the present Queen. It is *she* that must decide.'

Georgie sighed again. 'Well, I'll do my best, Lucia, but I really can't promise anything. The workings of Government are beyond me sometimes.'

Georgie had received more bad news earlier that month. His beloved Skylon was to be dismantled, together with most of the Festival of Britain buildings, supposedly in order to ease a national shortage of scrap metal. Churchill had ordered this as soon as he returned to Office and now the dreadful deed was about to be done. A polite letter had thanked Georgie for his contribution to the Festival project and informed him that he would soon be receiving a souvenir ashtray made from the main body of the Skylon as a lasting token of the event – a rather sad and undignified ending, thought Georgie.

The telephone rang in the hall and soon afterwards Grosvenor came through to the garden-room to ask whether Lady Pillson was free to speak to Mrs. Plaistow. 'She seems in a bit of a state, Ma'am. Seems that there has been an accident at the tea-shop. Something about the oven blowing up!'

'Goodness!' exclaimed Georgie as Lucia made her way to the telephone. 'Is she alright?'

'Just shock I think, Sir. But she's quite upset.'

'A loud bang… the door blew off… the electrics fused… anything else dear?' asked Lucia trying to make some sense of Diva's slightly incoherent and tearful narrative.

'And Janet says that she will never set foot into the kitchen again? I'm sure that she will calm down eventually, Diva dear. We are on our way over. Have a cup of sweet tea whilst you're waiting.'

Hastily, the Pillsons made their way to Wasters to be greated by a large notice posted on the door saying 'Tea-shop closed until further notice'. Through the window they could see Diva sat at a table, dabbing at her eyes with the edge of the tablecloth. Lucia thought it polite to knock and as she opened the door, Diva burst into tears.

'It's such a mess, Lucia,' sobbed Diva. 'I'm finished!'

'Nonsense!' retorted Lucia. 'A little set-back, perhaps, but we'll soon have you back in business.'

'Yes, we couldn't possibly live without your sardine tartlets!' added Georgie, trying his best to sound convincing.

'Now, shall we have a look in the kitchen?' asked Lucia.

Lucia had not been expecting to see the utter devastation that greeted her eyes. It was quite evident that the oven had indeed 'blown up'. Not only had the door been flung off its hinges, but shards of glass and pieces of twisted metal carpeted the floor. A gooey brown substance coated the kitchen walls creating an impression not dissimilar to one of Quaint Irene's early landscapes.

'Treacle pudding,' emitted Diva.

'Treacle pudding?'

'Tins of treacle pudding. Janet was heating the tins in the oven but forgot to pierce the lids.'

'But shouldn't they be boiled in a pan, Diva?' asked Lucia with a degree of certainty despite the fact that she had never prepared a treacle pudding herself.

'If you follow the instructions, Lucia but heating in the oven is quicker and more cost-effective.'

'Not if it ruins the whole kitchen,' added Georgie, whose comment caused Diva to begin crying all over again.

Taking charge of the situation, Lucia despatched Diva to her bedroom to have a lie down and then telephoned Mr.

Hardiman, the electrician who had served her since moving to Tilling. Both Grosvenor and Foljambe were called to begin clearing up the mess, for Janet was nowhere to be seen and would probably be in no fit state to undertake the task anyway, having been in the kitchen at the time of the explosion. Lucia had been assured by Diva that Janet had been left physically unscarred by the incident – though her state of mind may have taken somewhat of a knock.

Lucia could be heard saying 'How you all work me!' as she passed Grosvenor and Foljambe soapy cloths, towels and a mop.

Chapter 27

By the end of the week, the tea-shop was ready to open again for the week-end trade. As summer approached, the steady stream of tourists visiting Tilling and the surrounding area increased with a good number of them requiring sustenance, suitably provided by Diva's tea-shop. Lucia had asked Mr. Hardiman to find a new oven as soon as possible and he had come up trumps, finding an almost identical model which was surplus to requirements at a large hotel in Hastings which he had recently re-wired. The owner had sold it to Mr. Hardiman at a very reasonable price and Mr. Hardiman had made a handsome profit, earning an additional bonus from Lucia to boot.

Cadman and Foljambe were packing the last of their things into an assortment of cases and packing boxes that were laid upon the floor of the workshop. Too small in number to justify the hiring of a removal lorry, Lucia had given Cadman permission to use the Rolls-Royce to transport their belongings to Folkestone. It would only take two round journeys and after bringing the car back to Willows End, he would make the final journey to the coast by train. Lucia had given Cadman a handsome cheque as a parting gift and 'thank you' for all his years of service, which would go a long way in paying for the establishment of the Bed and Breakfast. Georgie had given Foljambe one of his most treasured bibelots – a miniature Art Deco Cartier silver and enamel desk clock which kept perfect time. Georgie had promised that he would visit soon but wasn't so sure that he would take advantage of the offer of either bed or breakfast.

Later on in the day, Lucia sat at her desk, perusing a small pile of letters written by the Royal hand. Reading it again, the first letter – penned just after Georgie's Investiture – seemed quite formal . But with each subsequent letter, the style became less so and might even be described as being rather chatty as Princess Elizabeth (later the Queen) wrote about events at the Palace, engagements she had attended, the exploits of her husband (which appeared to be many and varied) and her desire not to let the trappings of Royalty overshadow her everyday life as a young mother. Lucia had purchased a briefcase-sized wooden box made of burr walnut with a red velvet interior from Harrods on a recent trip to London in which to keep the letters. A sturdy lock and ornate key kept them away from any prying eyes.

Grosvenor entered.
'Ma'am, you have two visitors.'
'Really, Grosvenor? They are a little early but do bring them through.'
'Very well, Ma'am,' and Grosvenor returned with Milly, the hospital ancillary, and her husband – Mr. Alfred Miles, each carrying a large suitcase. They entered the room and Milly curtseyed to Lucia and Alfred bowed.
'I think that we can dispense with such formality, Milly – after all it *is* 1952!'
'If you are sure, Ma'am,' replied Milly.

'Absolutely! Now Grosvenor will show you to your accommodation above the workshop. I'm sure you will find that everything is in order. Foljambe made sure that the fridge was fully stocked before she left earlier today. Cadman is still here, however, packing his last trunk and will be able to show you the Rolls, Alfred. He will be catching a train to Folkesone shortly.'

'Perhaps I might transport him there by car, Ma'am?'

'An excellent suggestion, Alfred. I'm sure that Cadman will be most appreciative. You *have* driven a Rolls-Royce before?'

'Don't worry Ma'am. As long as it's got four wheels, an engine and some decent brakes, I'll be fine!' and he gave Lucia a beaming smile. Lucia noticed a slight twinkle in his eye which she found to be rather endearing.

'Sir George and I will discuss your duties tomorrow. Settle yourselves in today.'

Alfred peered through the workshop door. Cadman was polishing the front bumper of the Rolls, the chromework now positively gleaming.

'She's a beauty!' exclaimed Alfred as Cadman turned round to face the newcomer.

'She certainly is,' replied Cadman. 'Driving her is a sheer pleasure. Smooth as silk!'

Alfred approached Cadman.

'Alfred Miles. Lady Pillson's new chauffeur,' and he held out his hand. 'No need to take the train to Folkestone – I'll drive you there. You can give me a few pointers on the journey.'

'Well, that would be very helpful.'

'And I'll ask Milly to make us a cup of tea before we go.' Cadman immediately warmed to Alfred. He knew that Lucia would be in good hands which made his parting just a little easier.

Georgie had decided to visit the High Street and undertake a few errands in order to take his mind off the departure of Foljambe. He kept on reminding himself that she was only moving a few miles away. It wasn't as if she was emigrating to Australia! Though, truth be told, it felt just as bad. Foljambe had been by Georgie's side for so many years that she instinctively 'knew' and 'understood' his many needs, whims and foibles. Indeed, she had, without complaint, assisted Georgie on the journey from confirmed bacherlorhood to spouse – a word that Georgie particularly hated. He had purposely asked Lucia to never refer to him as such.

Georgie entered Twistevant's on a mission to find several dried ingredients for a particularly challenging recipe in Elizabeth David's *A Book of Mediterranean Food*. Georgie's culinary exploits in the War had brought him a brief period of celebrity but, following the cessation of hostilities, his interest had waned only to be sparked again by the preparations for Lucia's Grand Ball. Secretly, he had ordered David's book and intended to cook a special meal for Lucia – as near to a romantic gesture as he was prepared to undertake. In preparation, he had already been rather creative with olives one afternoon. Taking advantage of the fact that Lucia had left Willows End to meet with her accountant in London, he could now pit for England!

He showed Mr. Twistevant his neat hand-written list which prompted a noticeable raising of eyebrows.

'Not sure whether I have all this in stock at the moment, Sir, but I can certainly order it in for you.'

'That would be most acceptable, Twistevant,' replied Georgie who knew that the general store owner was always willing to bend over backwards for his best customers.

Next, Georgie visited the newly-opened Cooperative Chemists, prompted by an imaginative window display of pain-relieving creams and lotions with the legend *Suffer no more!* emblazoned above. Georgie's occasional twinges had become much more frequent as of late. Georgie's doctor had unhelpfully dismissed them as simply 'burdens of old age' which might be made more tolerable by a stiff drink or two. Georgie bought three different tubes of ointment and would try them in turn.

Finally Georgie made his way to see Mr. Hopkins, Tilling's fishmonger. If Lucia was to be successful in reviving the Royal Fish Express, there would need to be a ready supply of fish available for the Royal table. Hopkins always had a fine selection of freshly-landed *fruits de mer* for the good people of Tilling but Georgie was particularly interested in whether he had the means and wherewithal to supply the Palace where, Georgie assumed, vast quantities were needed for the State Banquets and other functions.

'Eels, Sir George?' enquired Hopkins.

'What about them?'

'I expect they'll be wanting a few of those as well. After all, those London folk are all well-eeled, aren't they, Sir?'

Georgie gave the customary laugh. Hopkins had a small but respectable repertoire of 'fish' jokes which regularly trotted out for the amusement of his customers.

'I believe King Henry the First died after eating a large plate of eels, Sir George,' continued Hopkins.

'How interesting, Hopkins,' replied Georgie, plainly not interested in the slightest, 'I'll be in touch,' and he left the jolly fishmonger to his gutting.

Georgie was now beginning to regret his decision to walk to the High Street as it necessitated an equally arduous walk back. The sky was beginning to darken and Georgie could hear a distant roll of thunder. He had left Willows End without a raincoat or umbrella, forgetting that the English weather can turn for the worst in an instant. As his journey progressed, the odd splats of rain became increasingly more intense and Georgie sought shelter under a large oak tree by the roadside. A flash of lightning signified the beginnings of a heavy downpour.

Alfred slowed down as the road surface became waterlogged and switched the headlights to full beam. He had taken Cadman to Folkestone and was now on his way back to Willows End. In the distance he could see a man sheltering rather unsuccessfully underneath a large tree to his left. Slowing down even further, Alfred could just make out the bedraggled features of his employer and pulled up alongside, beeping the horn.

'In you get, Sir. I'll soon have you home and comfortable.'

A very wet and somewhat distressed Georgie climbed into the back of the Rolls, emitting a huge sigh of relief.

'Not the best place to shelter in a thunderstorm, if you don't mind me saying so, Sir,' commented Alfred as he shifted from first to second gear.

Georgie did rather mind him saying so but remained silent.

'My Milly will get you a nice hot drink when we get back to Willows End, Sir and then she'll run you a steaming bath.'

But all Georgie really wanted was Foljambe.

Chapter 28

As another summer passed by, life in Tilling continued in its normally unremarkable fashion save for an unfortunate incident involving a vase of pink peonies and the Wyse's television set – the former unfortunately placed precariously upon the latter, with disastrous results. Mr. Wyse had forgotten to add the expensive device to his home insurance contents and thus a suitable payout was out of the question. 'We can always go round to the Mapp-Flints,' was his consoling reply to Susan's 'What are we going to do now, Algernon?'

It was six o' clock in the evening and Lucia and Georgie were preparing themselves for a visit to Grebe, where Quaint Irene was officially unveiling her Elizabethan mural, painted upon the dining room wall. The Wyses, Bartletts, Mapp-Flints and Godiva Plaistow had been invited alongside interested members of the press, the esteemed art critic Eric Newton and David Sylvester who had recently curated the first show of an up-and-coming artist named Henry Moore. Lucia had seen some of his work and had pronounced it 'transitory'. A Mr. Lennox from the National Trust had also been invited. Lucia had seen the work in progress but not the finished article. She was hopeful that Quaint Irene had not veered from her original design in too dramatic a fashion. Then again, Miss Coles was a law to herself and nothing, absolutely *nothing* could be ruled out!

At precisely seven o' clock, Alfred had the Rolls ready at the front steps of Willows End. He was wearing a smart dark green uniform and a chauffer's peaked cap which Georgie had decorated with a stylised 'W E' monogram on the front, using a fine silver thread. He held the rear doors open as Sir George and Lady Pillson climbed into the car, carefully checking that they were securely shut before setting off on the short ride to Grebe.

On arrival, a number of cars were already parked alongside the road leading up to Grebe. Over the summer months, the road had been widened and a small, sympathetically-designed car park was being constructed by the side of the house in order to facilitate visitor parking. Lucy stood on the front step, her six-foot frame an imposing sight, and handed out glasses of deep purple alcoholic punch, the contents being of mostly Russian origin.

The guests were mostly already assembled in the dining room where a large cotton bedsheet kept the mural from public view. Quaint Irene was in deep conversation with David Sylvester who was scribbling down copious notes in his diary. Two press photographers were helping themselves to egg and cress sandwiches.

Lucia had previously agreed to act as hostess for the evening and after a quick word with Irene, cleared her throat purposely.
'Ladies and gentleman,' she announced, 'It is both my duty and pleasure to welcome you to my former home,

Grebe, now gifted to the National Trust,' and she nodded in the direction of Mr. Lennox, who suitably nodded back.

'Almost immediately, I thought that there could be no one better than our dear Irene Coles to become the custodian of this wonderful house and restore it back to its former glory, following several years of neglect.'

Mapp squirmed internally at this veiled rebuke.

'And, characteristically, dear Irene has imprinted her own personality on these very walls. Ladies and gentleman, may I present.....*Elizabeth and her Muses,'* and she pulled the bedsheet from off the wall.

Inspired by Tintoretto's sixteenth-century masterpiece *The Muses,* Quaint Irene had depicted the new Queen lying asleep on a red chaise longue, a small crown angled obliquely upon her head. The nine daughters of Jupiter and Mnemosyne surrounded her – each one with an instantly recognisible face – Lucia, Georgie, Mapp, Benjy, Algernon and Susan Wyse, Rev. Bartlett and Evie and Diva. Apart from Lucia and Mapp who stood either side of the Queen, the other muses were hiding behind the couch, their heads peering over the top as they watched the sleeping monarch. Lucia held out a red rose and wrapped around Mapp's left hand was an adder, it's forked tongue clearly visible. The muses were all naked, though any possible offending parts of the anatomy were cleverly concealed by a combination of foliage and silken drapery. The mural was most certainly unconventional, rather daring but in no way disrespectful. Lucia breathed a sigh of relief.

There was a short hiatus as the image registered in the minds of the guests, followed by an appreciative round of applause and some animated chatter as those depicted compared likenesses.

'A masterpiece!' exclaimed Eric Newton. 'You are to be congratulated Miss Coles. Such an unusual composition but entirely appropriate. And full of deep symbolism, I believe.'

'Deep symbolism,' confirmed Lucia in her lowest possible tone. 'So glad to be the holder of the rose!'

'Who else could I entrust it to, my Angel?' replied Irene.

'And the snake wrapped around Mapp's hand?' enquired Georgie, making sure that Mapp was out of earshot.

'They slither around, spitting poison, ready to catch their next victim!' answered Irene, rather animatedly.

'What about the snake?' whispered Georgie, to Lucia's amusement.

The Mapp-Flints sidled up to the group now surrounding Irene.

'Such a charming likeness of my dear Benjy-boy, Quaint one,' effused Mapp. 'And my dear self, given a *starring* role alongside dearest Lucia!'

'Surely *that* belongs to the Queen?' chipped in Diva.

'Of course, Diva dear,' acquiesced Mapp.

'God bless her!' added the Major, raising his glass. 'This punch has quite a kick, Miss Coles!'

'Lucy's very own concoction, Major. All sorts of things went into it – most of them legal!' and she grabbed hold of a glass, just as the maid passed by, tray in hand.

'Quai hai, Major!' trumpeted Irene, and promptly emptied the glass with one large glug.

'Quai hai!' repeated the Major and downed the rest of his drink to the horror of his wife. She had been carefully counting his alcoholic intake and this was his fourth glass of the evening.

'Steady on, Benjy!' she whispered. 'No more punch for you!'

'Of course, Liz-girl,' he replied, whilst giving Lucy, who stood nearby, a rather obvious wink.

The night was warm and Lucia stepped out of the house and wandered into the garden where the view of the salt marshes was uninterrupted and the smell of the sea was pungent. She could hear the waves, crashing in the distance, bringing back memories of the terrible flood.

'Lucia! Lucia are you there?'

Georgie had seen Lucia pass by the window several minutes ago and, having not returned to the house, wondered if she was feeling well.

'Over here Georgie,' replied Lucia, waving her arm in the fading light. 'Just getting a spot of fresh air and…. remembering, Georgie.'

'Oh Lucia!' sympathised Georgie, whose guilt at thinking her drowned all those years ago had never waned.

He took hold of her hand and gave her a gentle kiss, taking comfort in the fact that during such rare moments of frailty, *she* needed *him*.

Chapter 29

Lucia was unusually nervous. She had managed to eat a slice of toast for breakfast but could face little else. This was the day that she had dreamed about for so many years and everything just *had* to go well.

'Georgie! Are you ready yet?' Lucia called. Georgie had already tried on three outfits and blamed the absence of Foljambe for his indecision.
'We need to leave here in twenty minutes – the timings are quite precise!' and she called for Grosvenor to check that Alfred was preparing the Rolls.

A few minutes later, Georgie came down the stairs – Milly following closely behind. With her encouragement he had settled on a three piece tweed suit, a dark burgundy silk tie and fedora, which he held in his hand.
'Georgino mio!' cried Lucia. 'Such style and sophistication!' and she squeezed his arm encouragingly. 'Let me just adjust your Insignia….'

Outside Willows End, Alfred sounded the horn of the Rolls-Royce, indicating that he was all ready to transport its owners into Tilling. However, as he opened the rear doors, ready to accept Lucia and Georgia, he stumbled on the kerb and fell to the ground. A little dazed but unhurt he began to get up but noticed that his prosthetic lower limb had become detached – as it was prone to do occasionally. Fortunately, his curses were uttered before

Lady Pillson passed through the front door of Willows End.

'Oh dear, Alfred!' exclaimed a concerned Lucia. 'Are you alright?'
'Yes, Ma'am. Perfectly fine. But I'll have to fix my leg. I can't reach the clutch pedal without it.'
Lucia saw the lower limb by a flower bed, clearly in need of some repair.
'Haven't had a fall for months, Ma'am. Trust it to be today of all days! But don't you worry – I'll soon have it fixed,' and he hobbled to the workshop, assisted by Milly. An able-bodied man would have, at this point, received a severe tongue-lashing from Lucia but the absence of Alfred's lower left leg was hardly his fault.

Red, white and blue bunting decorated Tilling Station and waved in the warm breeze alongside a plethora of hanging baskets, full to the brim with late summer flowers. It seemed that the whole of Tilling was crowded onto the platform, the Mapp-Flints, Wyses, Bartletts, Diva and even Quaint Irene (who had declared herself an ardant Republican at the mural unveiling after consuming too many glasses of Lucy's punch) standing at the front. The train would be arriving at ten o' clock sharp and Lucia and Georgie were nowhere to be seen. The Mayor of Tilling, Mr. Clemments, looking resplendent with his gold chain of office, was nervously checking his pocket watch. Sir George and Lady Pillson should have arrived at least ten mintes ago.

Soon after, in the distance, the advancing train could be heard as it thundered along the tracks, plumes of smoke puffing high into the sky. The Mayor checked his watch yet again.

'Where on earth is Lucia, Benjy?' asked Mapp. 'The train's about to arrive and the Mayor is perspiring very heavily. He doesn't look at all well.'

'Not like Lady Pillson to be late, Liz-girl. You don't think something untoward has happened?' replied the Major.

Diva nudged Mapp.

'This could be a disaster, Elizabeth. Lucia's left us in the lurch!'

The train slowed down as it approached the Station and blew its piecing whistle. There was a expectant hush on the platform as the engine came to a halt and the door of the single carriage opened. The Mayor nervously stepped forward to greet the Queen as she stepped out of the train and there was a loud cheer from the crowd and enthusiastic waving of Union Jack flags.

'So pretty in the flesh!' commented Quaint Irene, who had used, of all things, a postage stamp likeness for her Elizabethan mural.

The Mayor appeared to be whispering something into the Queen's ear causing a frown to appear on the Royal brow. Mapp could see that the Mayor was beginning to flounder and – as an ex-Mayoress of Tilling – it was her duty to try and relieve the situation. In a flash, she hurdled over the rope barrier and strode purposely towards the Queen, curtseying as low as she was able. Following a brief word with the Mayor, Elizabeth addressed the Queen.

'Your Majesty, I believe that proceedings may be delayed for a short while and might I most humbly suggest we visit my dear ancestral home – Mallards House – where light refreshments are available. It is just around the corner!' and she grabbed the Mayor's arm and marched off in the direction of Mallards. The Queen and her small entourage had no option but to follow, to the dismay of the crowd.

'One lump or two, Ma'am?' enquired Mapp. 'Milk or cream? Perhaps a fruit scone or jam puff – all freshly baked by my own hand this very morning?'

The Queen drank her tea, served in Mapp's finest china but declined anything to eat.

'Perhaps you may like to wander amongst the Roman Ruins?' asked Mapp. 'They are of national importance – but I am sure you are well aware of that.'

Withers entered, relaying the news that Sir George and Lady Pillson had now arrived at the Station and the ceremony could begin proper.

'Before you go, Ma'am, may I present you with a little gift – just to remember your stay at Mallards?' and she removed one of her own paintings from the wall, passing a small study of apples in a delft bowl to the Queen.

The Queen looked at the picture for just a moment.

'Thank you, Mrs. Mapp-Flint. I know *exactly* where I shall put it!'

'The crowd's becoming restless, Lucia,' whispered Georgie as he stood by his wife alongside the engine, awaiting the return of the Royal party.

'I'm sure that their good nature will return as soon as the Queen arrives back,' replied Lucia, calmly. 'Oh look! Here they come now!'

As they got closer, Lucia noticed with dismay that the Royal party now appeared to include the Mapp-Flints. A beaming Mapp walked alongside the Queen, with the Major in tow, just behind. Lucia curtseyed and Georgie bowed as the Queen joined them on the platform. She gave Lucia a broad smile and…. was that the slightest of winks?

'It gives me great pleasure to name this train the Royal Fish Express!' and the Queen removed the small sash that had been covering the nameplate to reveal the legend, cast in brass. There was another round of applause and three cheers were called for Her Majesty. Mr. Hopkins then appeared in pristine whites, carrying a wicker basket of freshly caught fish which was duly accepted by one of the gentlemen accompanying the Queen. An official photographer then captured the scene for posterity – to be printed in all the national newspapers later on in the week. She then promptly returned to her carriage, waved to the onlookers and the Royal Fish Express pulled out of the Station, cheered on by the crowd.

The Royal Fish Express was to have a purely ceremonial function, delivering fish from Tilling to London (from where it would be transported to the Palace in a horse-drawn carriage accompanied by a Yeoman from the Royal Household) on the feast day of Saint Peter – the patron Saint of fishermen. For the rest of the year, the Royal Fish Express would be used by British Railways, servicing the general transport needs of the London Midland region. Georgie had met twice with Mr. Lennox-Boyd who had dismissed Lucia's idea entirely at first but had been persuaded to bring the matter to the attention of the Queen provided that all costs relating to the painting of a new livery for the engine and casting of a new nameplate (for the locomotive was to be one already in service) would be met by Sir George and Lady Pillson themselves. Georgie had readily agreed.

That evening, Willows End was the venue for a Celebration Dinner. The Mayor had been invited but, following the stresses of the day, had sent word that he was unfortunately feeling rather under the weather and sadly would not be attending. Thus the guests consisted of the Wyses, Mapp-Flints, Bartletts, Diva and Quaint Irene (who promised to remain tea-total for the evening).

'Couldn't resist asking for one of my little piccies,' Mapp informed Diva. 'I hadn't the heart to refuse, dear! Such a chatterbox too!'

Lucia listened to the conversation with a sense of both disbelief and indignation. She should have realised that Mapp would take the fullest advantage possible of what was, after all, a purely chance meeting with Her Majesty.

'What did she say, Mapp? Do tell!' probed Diva.

'Well, I was sworn to secrecy, but she did let slip….'

Lucia decided to check the progress of dinner.

What better dish to celebrate the day's events than *Lobster à la Riseholme*? Mr. Hopkins had included a couple of the magnificent crustaceans in the wicker basket he had presented earlier, but had reserved the prize specimens for Lady Pillson's dinner party. All agreed that Lucia's culinary creation tasted even better this evening.

Collective eyes were on Georgie as he rose from his seat and gingerly tapped his wine glass. Prompted by Lucia, he had prepared a short speech, praising her efforts in reviving the Royal Fish Express.

'...And finally – please raise your glasses. Three cheers for Lucia! Hip hip hooray! Hip hip....'

The guests had left and Georgie had finally retired upstairs. Everything was – at least for the moment – calm and still. A perfect time for Lucia to reflect.

Such a lot had changed in recent times since she had awoken from her coma. Amongst other things she had acquired a title, moved from Mallards to Willows End, become a benefactress to the Nation, waved goodbye to Cadman and Foljambe and developed a growing friendship with Queen Elizabeth.

Yet, she was still a confirmed Tillingite, Georgie a constant presence by her side, surrounded by a somewhat eccentric but irreplaceable circle of friends – Mapp included! She chuckled to herself – she would have it no other way!

Your favourite characters will appear next in:

Treasure Mapp

The Author

Ian Shepherd is Head of Expressive Arts at a Norfolk academy, where he teaches music.

He studied at Sheffield University, winning the Music Dissertation Prize and completed post-graduate studies at Bretton Hall College, Wakefield. It was at this time that he 'discovered' E. F. Benson's *Mapp and Lucia* books.

He is the author of *The Drawing Room Symphony – A History of the Piano Duet Transcription*. In it, the observant reader will find a reference to Lucia and Georgie's *po di musica*!